ANA GLORIA MOYA

Heaven of Drums

Translated by W. Nick Hill

CURBSTONE PRESS

A Lannan Translation Selection
with Special Thanks to Patrick Lannan and
the Lannan Foundation Board of Directors

FIRST ENGLISH EDITION, 2007
Copyright © 2007 by Ana Gloria Moya
Translation copyright © 2007 by W. Nick Hill
All rights reserved.

Printed on acid-free paper
Cover design by Susan Shapiro.
Cover painting: Portrait of a Negress, 1799-1800; oil on canvas by
Benoist, Marie Guilhelmine (1768-1826).
© Louvre, Paris, France / The Bridgeman Art Library.
Printed in Canada

This book was published with the support of the Connecticut
Commission on Culture and Tourism, The Connecticut State
Legislature through the Office Of Policy and Management,
The Lannan Foundation, and donations from many individuals.
We are very grateful for this support.

We also thanks Jane Blanshard for her copy-editing help.

Library of Congress Cataloging-in-Publication Data

Moya, Ana Gloria, 1954-
  [Cielo de tambores. English]
  Sky of drums / Ana Gloria Moya ; translated by W. Nick Hill. —
1st ed.
     p. cm.
  ISBN-13: 978-1-931896-25-2 (pbk. : alk. paper)
  ISBN-10: 1-931896-25-9 (pbk. : alk. paper)
  I. Hill, W. Nick, 1944- II. Title.
  PQ7798.23.O847C5413 2006
  863'.64—dc22

                              2006019344

published by
    CURBSTONE PRESS   321 Jackson Street   Willimantic, CT 06226
          phone: 860-423-5110   e-mail: info@curbstone.org
                        www.curbstone.org

Translator's Acknowledgments

A wise man has said that in this work two heads are better than one. I wish to thank Barbara Arnn for always being the second, clearer head. I want to thank Sandy Taylor, whose keen editorial sense almost bites sometimes. My thanks also to Drew Hill for checking texts, and to David Brown for knowledge of plants. To Carolyn Kost for her language expertise and her research ability. And to José María de Freitas, Ivana Brighenti, and Marcelo Rodríguez for help with interesting words and phrases that I would like to call Argentinisms. If there are others who should be acknowledged, that omission is innocent, though entirely my responsibility, as is any egregious error of language or concept.

—W. Nick Hill

"To what heaven of drums and long siestas have they gone? Time has carried them off, time that is oblivion."

—Jorge Luis Borges

"Woman, you quiet adversary, in the mysterious custody of puzzling deaths. With a millenarian sound beating in the veins in your temples where a change of guard is almost imperceptible."

—Pablo Antonio Cuadra

To María Inés Loyola and Leonor Rosas Villada,
sisters in my truths and contradictions.

Preface

My name is Gregorio Rivas and, today, when the passage of time has tempered the strength of my passions, I begin writing this so the truth won't be lost in darkness. So that other bell, the one that tolls muffled by the official story, can be heard by all of you. I hope it's not too late.

September is a pitiless month for old folks. The scent of orange blossoms becomes arrogant and nothing can keep it from filtering in, through the cracks in the doors or into memory. It churns up the order that after great effort I had imposed on my feelings, and it demands the truth once and for all. In no way did the writing of so many fictions serve me to avoid the arrival of the moment to take stock of my life. I will die without heirs, and these memories are my way to persist. In a hundred years, with luck, perhaps some unsuspecting person will bring me back to life by reading what I write so desperately today.

You need to know who the woman was I loved most and the man I most hated. The end is approaching and I'm not sad. My feelings were as intense as my life. I never lost the passion to reach beyond my grasp, a little bit beyond my hopes.

These memoirs might seem to be the vanity natural to a writer who begins them convinced that no one will be able to do this better than he can. Perhaps that is true. But until now no one has known about the weighty memories I've kept hidden.

I want to tell you about realities that no one tried to understand, not even those who lived through this history. I'll set aside my natural tendency to go to extremes and promise to describe what took place just as it occurred.

But please do not imagine that the intensity of my feelings won't seep into these lines. Love and hate are the forces that move life; at times you hate the one you love, at times you love the one you hate. I never discovered the difference.

Heaven of Drums

ONE

I perfected in myself the difficult art of surviving as a minority

I was born in April of 1770 in the district of San Miguel de Tucumán in the province of Salta, when it was a poorly laid-out town of some five or six blocks. My father, Francisco Rivas, in a rapture of love that he regretted all his life, married the perfect, but illegitimate, product of the union of a Spaniard and an Indian, my mother.

I said that he soon regretted his impulse because his businesses very quickly prospered and the burden of my mother's race became an impediment to his desire to climb the social ladder.

It was such a grievous curse for my father that, as an act of love, she decided to die during her last childbirth, leaving his third male child in his arms, my brother Bernardo, the only one he loved. At least that's what his hand, whose touch I never felt, allowed me to conjecture when it played with my brother's hair. Neither Ignacio, the second-born, nor I ever knew him to manifest a weakness such as a tender touch.

His unquestionable command was that, as the firstborn, I should take over his businesses and elevate the Rivas name as high as the rigid society of that time would permit a half-breed to do. Ignacio, the least compromised in terms of skin color, found an indisputable way to elude our father's demands. He entered the seminary, less for a vocation than to satisfy his desire to travel far away and, as an ordained priest with brilliant marks, he went direct to the Vatican from there. Thus, he liberated himself from the paternal oppression that was inflicted on Bernardo. That poor soul grew up without a mother, in a house full of silent men and women who surreptitiously doled out pitying caresses. So he was never able to fortify himself for life and its pitfalls.

Francisco Rivas was the owner of the largest mule herds in the region. Merchants from Upper Peru or from Buenos Aires would come to buy the animals we raised. Even though many died, broken under the excessive weight of their cargo, the mules served as the merchants' only means to cross the difficult terrain all the way from the port of Callao to Buenos Aires. It was an excellent business, since the pastures in Tucumán were as generous as the land and in winter and in summer the mules grew fat from the daily free banquet. The only threat to the troopers' business was the danger of yellow spleen, a plague so contagious that if only one animal fell sick, the drovers, with their knives and their remorse, had to slaughter all the rest. No sacrifice was too small to venture to the coasts to transport the coveted merchandise from Europe.

My father's estate grew to such an extent that, needing to multiply his earnings, he bought up enormous cane fields in Trancas that exuded sugar if you merely looked at them. Some time later, the barrels filled with cane liquor were consumed in that region in such numbers that we Rivas were responsible for more than one crime in cheap dives and general stores where the liquor unleashed passions and hatred.

In the face of so much prosperity, and given Ignacio's rapid escape to Europe, from where we were convinced he would never return, Francisco Rivas decided to give me the best education possible so I could follow in his footsteps. In spite of my many furious tears, and my scant twelve years of age, he sent me to the Real Colegio de San Carlos in Buenos Aires.

For four years I perfected myself not only in theology, philosophy, and Latin grammar, but also in the difficult art of surviving as a minority. A dark minority, object of much ridicule...

From the first day of class, Manuel Belgrano and I were united by an intense hatred. Because I was a quiet provincial

2

and my feet were encased in poorly-made shoes, he believed he could order me to sit on the bench furthest to the rear. His black eye supplied me with my first penance, one that I happily paid for and that sealed our eternal enmity.

He realized that I suffered from not being close to Tucumán. He always had the ability to detect the miseries of others. He looked down on me because of my mixed blood, as fervently as I hated him for his blond hair and blue eyes. He lost no opportunity to humiliate me in front of our schoolmates. "Shitty Indian," he would yell at me, and my face would flush with rage. "Little blond dummy," I yelled back, imitating his high-pitched voice. And he went from white to red. He tried to hide it, but he could never fool me with his overacted role as melancholy altar boy *you acted like a saint in mass and everyone believed you not me you never tricked me I saw what you and your friends did at night under blankets in the darkened dormitories brown-nose, gossipy pig always snitching on us the worst was you laughing and enjoying the whippings Padre Anselmo gave us when you told him we smoked those stinky cigars in the baths I still have marks on my back from those nights when he would strip us and whip us in his cell while he made us recite ten Our Fathers as he panted and panted.*

On my return to Tucumán at Christmas, after fifteen days of fretful travel in a coach, my father examined my progress during the year, which he took care not to approve. He never forgave me for my Indian face that his blood had never managed to make as white as my brothers' faces. I was the darkest, the one truest to my mother's heritage. He never knew that my strength came from that.

By the April I turned fifteen, Francisco Rivas had married again, this time the corpulent white daughter of an Andalusian merchant, finally achieving his desired status as an upstanding member of the community. They had two daughters with whom I never shared a word, a path, or a glance.

In despair at the invasion of so much feminine bulk, he obstinately tried to get me started in the business and he would take me out into the rows of sugarcane to supervise the workers. But his efforts came late, as writing had already overpowered me with an intensity equal to his rejection, and I was never able to cure myself of it. It had begun to make me its prey as soon as I learned to read, guided by my mother's dear dark finger that pointed out the letters written with chalk on a blackboard she shared with me on her knees. In that way, leaving behind the soft woolen-handed fairy and the iron-fisted fairy, the siestas of my childhood in Tucumán became populated with words which, united with other words, kept me captive forever.

Later, with no order or plan, I began to secretly devour books that I sneaked out of the paternal library under my clothes. So it was that I left the works of Seneca, Virgil, and Petrarch sealed with candle wax and the salt of my tears. Nights became shorter and my permanently bloodshot eyes revealed the nocturnal vices that kept me awake.

The volcano erupted suddenly. The itch to write arose in me with such force that it made my hand clumsy, always trying to catch up to the ecstatic universes my mind gave birth to. Reality was insufficient and I needed to organize it in writing according to my whim. It was less painful that way.

For a period of more than three years after I left the College of San Carlos for good, my father had me take over the Rivas and Sons branch in Buenos Aires. The pretext of the ideals of equality and fraternity, recently arrived from France, brought a bunch of us together every night around café tables, from which we never could get up before sunrise and didn't want to, soaked in wine and dreams. No one in the city could find our store open in the morning hours, as likewise none could convince me that I should wait behind the counter—me, who the morning before was writing with the blood of all the drunks then present (of those who allowed their fingers to be pricked, in reality) the manifestoes we were sure would change the course of history.

The unfortunate business couldn't withstand my zeal for poetic jargon or the poetry of gambling, and I took it to the verge of bankruptcy. I don't know if I made an earnest effort to succeed, or if I forced myself to fail. Nature can't be twisted. It always imposes itself, far beyond reason.

When Franciso Rivas discovered that my heritage was superior to his strength, he decided that it was time to have one less son, and without the ceremony of a funeral, he buried me in a resentful oblivion.

He refused to hear explanations, nor did I wish to give any. When Bernardo found himself in the presence of the violent outbursts we exchanged, he cried with grief in a corner. I took advantage of a mule caravan that was departing for Lima, the city of delights, and with no more luggage than my fury, I left Tucumán.

That June 1770, María Kumbá and Manuel Belgrano were born in the midst of the joy of gods, black and white

From childhood on, María was a righteous mulatto, a dark whirlwind, an incessant zephyr, her father's caprice. She always bubbled over with generous laughter.

Her long-suffering mother gave birth to her that melancholy autumn in a corner of the great kitchen, with her lips pressed tightly closed to not let escape a howl of pain in the presence of the lacerating bolt of lightning that split her up the middle from the inside. Or to not cry out the forbidden name of the master who had had her in an unguarded moment, while already forgetting her. All sweat and pride, from the minute she placed the baby on her belly, palpitating and warm with blood, by means of a millenarian mandate the baby came to be incarnated as a warrior from the North for this savage, haughty place in the South. Her mother would see the birth of the warrior and would love her with all the force of her heart. She was baptized María. Her mother wanted her own mother's name for her. But the unequivocal order came from the priest's mouth: "It will be María, like the Mother of the Lord." When she found out, the only spark of rebellion in her life touched her, and that night, when everyone was asleep, she wrapped the baby up in a blanket and stealthily took her to Mama Basilia who lived near the river and was an Iyalorishá in the Yoruba tradition. Mama Basilia took the baby in her arms, she looked attentively at her as at an accomplice, and after freeing her from the clothing that trapped her, deposited her on the ground. She began to sing, dolefully invoking the distant Orishás in the middle of a cold June night. She did so with her arms in the air while she walked around the newborn who looked happy in her unexpected freedom, kicking her legs gleefully.

The gods heard her and were pleased to come down to

present her with their gifts, at which point the old woman fell down beside her with a cry and began to thank them: "Obtalá accepts her as his daughter, and she will be a brave woman, and many will speak of her. For him she will be named Kumbá."

Her mother proudly wrapped her up again and left quickly to return to the house, with the sure steps of one who has just given birth to a person selected by the family of gods.

A mulatto, she was the suckling sister of the other legitimate, fair daughter, to whom she was tied by the master's lust and the generosity that sprang from the breast of her mother who, sheepishly, would live in the shadow of the family that bought her until the day of her death, still pining for that African land where she would have been a princess.

It was a pleasure to see them run together in their child's world, distanced from everything that wasn't a game, under the shade of ancient trees in the patio like noon and midnight of a time that was gestating the change of a continent. And Ronda-Catonga and Tengue-Tengue were tirelessly repeated in their everyday sounds. Even at that young age the impulse that the mix of races gave her to ignore her status as a slave was apparent. Aloof, she directed the children's games her sister submitted to with pleasure because under her orders both danger and fun were assured. Until an alarmed adult cried out at the sight of heads rising above the top of some tree and put an end to the diversion, and then each one would return to her universe of origin: one to the parlor, the other to the kitchen.

What a pleasure to watch how she was transformed when the distant, nostalgic sounds of drums, mazacayas, and marimbas from some nighttime ceremony filtered through the silent house. At that instant her little body began to move rhythmically and gracefully to the beat of the music that invited dancing, like a messenger from another place.

She would close her eyes, and her arms and legs took on a life of their own, as though responding to an atavistic message, and they became her grandmothers who danced on the red tiles of the covered walkway. Her sister tried to imitate her in vain: she swayed her blond head and the difference did add some charm. But then, powerless to imitate her sister, she began to cry, so some adult would save her from the difference.

A mysterious one, María would disappear at times to seek the company of the little mulattoes in the neighboring house. There, sisters in secrets and the blood, they tried out naïve enchantments with clumsy magic rituals such as they had seen performed on servant girls in the kitchen who wanted a lover. They never knew if the death of brown Thomas, hated for his disloyalty and lustfulness, on a night of a full moon, was due to his habit of fishing while drunk or to their own invocation of all the Ajogún, their faces painted with ashes.

It was such associations that bound her to the dark forces of her religion, in which her mother secretly instructed her, that when folks got together after chores to say the rosary, she managed to harmonize those forces with that one bountiful God and His Mother, after whom she was named. She never did achieve a complete agreement between them and her intimate, living Orishás, but she did manage for them to live together peacefully, on every occasion invoking each one distinctly, as needed.

And so María Kumbá grew up, joining together the two bloods that flowed in her veins to give her the most beautiful share of each: white and black, black and white, a perfect combination that began to mark a presence in this viceroyalty yet being built, which would mark with flames the seal of African heritage.

**Oyá, warrior of the wind,
let not our country be invaded by destroyers.
Help me to rest on the earth, free of
unmerited deceptions.**

*Lordy, the ghosts are sure coming out to call on me tonight!
I ought to be jest about getting ready to die, or death ought
to be walking around on account of wanting to take me away.
That's what my grandmother would say when the time's come.
That the dead you love in life help you to die. And she did die
too, after so much pleading with Oyá to take her with him.
So pretty that poor little thing, she died of shame having to
go around with her forehead branded by an iron, just like an
animal. And one morning, all dressed in white, we saw her
staring up at the sky. For certain Old Boney doesn't frighten
me. I had him dogging my trail for so many years that if he
crowds me a bit, I'll jest say I want to die right now. I almost
don't recognize the living. With so many I loved waiting for
me, I want to be with them and not here, listening to Carmen
snore. Such a grump, she doesn't seem to be my
granddaughter.*

*My, it is hot tonight! Even worse with so much humidity;
the bugs fly around in clouds. I better stay sitting here in this
hammock where my bones suffer less than on that willow cot
to wait for it to get light. Not even with my cane can I move
around without everything hurting me, right down to my
nails.*

*Besides, what didn't I do in this life! I commenced to
fight beside my Sir Genrul at over 40 years of age. And I
never shrank from it, not even when they got a hold of me up
there at the North, not even when I was ironing that passel of
uniform shirts on account of the dandy little officers liked to
be well dressed. When the weather changes, I go around
creaking like a rusty hinge, what's a body to do! The years
don't ask permission, coming on little by little, driving death
ahead of 'em.*

This afternoon they dragged me out of Governor Viamonte's house again. I'm not going to see him anymore. The servants probably don't even want to tell him I'm looking for him. The poor thing, how happy he was when he recognized me! It was a Sunday and it occurred to me to go to the cathedral to wait for all those people to come out of 12-o'clock mass. It's the best place to ask for a few coins because they all leave saintly and generous. They believe that on account of blessing themselves on Sunday with holy water, they going to get to heaven...

Am I ashamed to beg? Truth is, not any more. I don't know hardly anybody who can save himself by being a beggar when money's no interest to him. If you don't believe me, look at my poor Sir Genrul. Pleading for help from the rich people, he came on all fours, throwing up blood, to die in Buenos Aires. They threw alms at him so he could pay for the trip! How could I, an old mulatto, save myself from that end, if even he couldn't!

Well, I'm going to keep on telling you how old Viamonte found me. That Sunday I was telling about, a nice, elegant gentleman coming out of the cathedral approached me. Sort of playing the fool, well, not that much, because sometimes my princess grandmother scolds me when she sees me being a pesky beggar. Jest then I feel someone grab my hand and say to me: "If it isn't Tía María!" The man was almost crying he became so emotional. I said to him: "I'm fine, I'm fine, don't you worry," and I patted him like before when we waited for the enemy in the middle of the night, and him shivering at death. You men should never be too confident, even the bravest ones get runny noses. Haven't I wiped their noses before and after battles!

Right there on the spot Governor Viamonte dismissed all the trooper boys who escorted him. He commenced to tell me what an injustice it was I had to go begging on the street, owing as how I was a soldier of Independence. I broke out laughing then and there because I was never a soldier. I was

*Tía María for all my boys, for my Sir Genrul, my Sir Genrul...
I can't remember him but what my eyes, all by themselves,
start weepin'.*

*An old woman's sniffles, Carmen says. But I don't cry
for no reason because I've seen for sure all that saintly soul
suffered, suffered like I never seen the like, and if he strayed
in some way it was in loving the country too much and
forgetting to love himself. I'm telling you all this, who knew
him, who loved him like nobody else, I swear to you, and
even though it won't ever be known... Well, mind if I'm not a
big-mouth, I'm not even acquainted with you, and I was all
ready to let loose the heaviest secret I keep in my heart.*

*Tonight the stars seem like lanterns, jest like up North.
What country up there! Pretty places, full of people so brave
at the hour of battle they seemed half-crazed, with some
warrior Orishá guiding them from inside. A person comes
down those narrow canyons almost falling off her mule, and
I tell you it seems the mountain is going to squash you. But
no, down below, the flatland waits for you, and it goes on
until you begin to climb another colorful mountain as red as
if it was angry waiting there in the distance. Over there they
bunch up together and rise up mighty high, snow or clouds
the same, depending on the season of the year.*

*I tell you the boys would laugh to see my fear. The look
on my face made them laugh out loud, accustomed as I was
to Buenos Aires that doesn't even have one single little hill.
The one who laughed the most was Gregorio Rivas, that
shameless lech who had my clothes off before I even realized
it. My boys, their faces also visit me tonight, like you.... A
day doesn't go by that I don't ask Oyá to keep their souls. So
young and brave, my heart still aches to remember how they
kept up-and-dying on me. Tacuarí, Salta, Ayohuma, all of it
gets all tangled up in this old head that can't forget about
them either. When will the fright of those memories leave me
be?*

TWO

Life slipped away from us as we inarticulately asked for help

I should confess that my initiation into the pleasures of the flesh came late because of distractions. When I noticed I was already 18 and had never touched or seen a naked woman, I closed the book I was reading. The moment had come to leave behind the solitary pleasures and prove whether feminine geography coincided with the fiery descriptions in my readings.

I did not search for long. I was surrounded by candidates desirous of feeling the hands of the patrón's son on their hot, voluminous hips. A Tucumán siesta, a canebrake, and my clumsiness yoked together two perspiring bodies that hardly looked at each other, urged on by impatient desire. I do not recall her face, much less her name, but from that day until my return to Buenos Aires, she was my breakfast along with orange juice and the thick coffee that each morning I took to my bedroom.

Of course there were other women with lust as unbridled as mine, whom I possessed in moist, fevered beds. But time passed and, in spite of my dedication to know the story of love in full bloom, I only knew about it through reading, and that wasn't enough. Everything changed when María burst into my life so late that I had already resigned myself to ignorance. I had never revealed the heights and depths that always inhabited me and it was only to her that I dared to make a confession. From her I learned that being orphaned from the beloved's taste and smell can even kill.

I had barely arrived when Lima captured me in her colorful fingers. The City of Kings stretched languidly there along the banks of the Rimac. For young men it was well known as the Earthly Paradise, a mix of Sodom and Gomorrah that promised prohibited pleasures in the hands of avid, lusty women. It was said that everything was joyfully permitted, and I headed there, dragging along my status as a prodigal son with no intention of being redeemed.

I adjusted myself quite naturally to the pulsing, erotic rhythm of that brash picturesque city. I carried a letter of introduction from my distant relative and true friend, Cornelio Saavedra. It opened the doors to Lima society for me and soon I was just one more of those young men, university students on the whole, who had already begun to question their century-old servility to the Spanish crown. The Limeños fascinated me by simply assuming they had mixed blood. They were quite proud of their heritage, so different from us, whose sense of identity was always mixed up. There were few who pined for lighter-colored skin, and my new friends bent the branches of their genealogical tree in order to brush against Manco Capac. With naïve vanity for their courtly life full of glitter copied from Madrid's, the older people dressed in velvet to stroll along streets where chariots of gold bumped into mounds of manure on every corner.

I was given such a solid fraternal welcome that in less than two weeks of my arrival, thanks to Saavedra's intro-duction and influence, I was enveloped in two of the most intoxicating aromas I ever knew: the smell of ink and paper. It could well be that my joining *El Mercurio Peruano*, the most important periodical in the Viceroyalty, was due to indifference cheered on by the need to survive, though soon its rhythm drew me in. Then, as in previous times, that old volcano erupted and fused my writing with journalism, a new vice much like passion.

I began my job in a dark corner of the building and ended up as its director for almost ten years. I discovered the erotic sensation of being read barely two days after giving birth to the ideas. The publication was irregular on many occasions, but assembling its lively chaotic contents, in which satires of the viceroy and the bishop were mixed up with notices of recent news from Europe, was a challenge I never regretted.

My Limeño friends were idealists and revolutionaries who years later would make up the ruling class in this disorderly, savage America. In whatever drinking establishment full of smoke and liquor we found ourselves, the brilliance and bombast of our discussions about literature and politics rivaled each other. Literature and politics, thought and action, beginning and end. Already drunk as a skunk, who can extract himself from the fruitless pleasure of putting the world to rights at a table in a café!

My pride in being an American continued to grow there, and I forever lost that dark shame of my Indian blood. It was unnecessary to imitate Europeans in order to exist. We had our own identity, we had only to describe it.

For that reason, when they learned that my undying enemy, Manuel Belgrano, exchanged letters with Princess Carlota Joaquina in which he declared himself to be her most loyal subject, I became a laughingstock. That pathetic creature, always dreaming of monarchies! *and envying European family lines you showed it a mile away you were ashamed of being the son of a somewhat poor merchant with a brood of children so many times I heard you curse your bad luck for having been born here you were so annoying to your parents that they became fed up and saved enough money to send you to Salamanca that way you had the pleasure of feeling European less Indian whiter you lackey little lackey*

The most reckless of us, for a bribe of only a few coins, gained access to French Revolutionary publications, prohibited by the local Inquisition, that clandestinely entered through the port of Callao. Thanks to my position at *El Mercurio,* I could deceive the censor and fondle those "prohibited books" that arrived from Europe. But when the money for vices was scarce, the wiles we resorted to were as ingenious as they were ridiculous. Just plotting them was a

well-recompensed diversion that we would not have missed
for anything in the world. A cask of wine, a hatbox, or a large
soutain, it was all game for tricking port security and for
feeding the soul.

That was how Rousseau, Diderot, Montesquieu came
into my possession. The phrase "the people" became charged
for me with a concrete, workable meaning. I began to find a
place to belong.

I spent the pleasantest years of my life in Lima. My
voluntary exile served to deepen my affections and my
hatreds. Once in a while I would receive a visit from an old
classmate, who would come with his high ideals or his base
lasciviousness, and no matter what his baggage, he returned
satisfied. For them I stayed abreast of the gossip in that
southern port which began to boil with contradictions,
beginning in 1800. They twice repulsed English attempts to
invade and began to nurse the idea of getting Spain off their
back, too.

The only tie that bound me to Tucumán was my
correspondence with Bernardo. He wrote to me with the
regularity of a heartbeat. It was asphyxiating him to remain
the sole repository of our father's weighty hopes, but his
weak, good-natured character would not let him claim his
own space in life. What's more, I think he never knew he had
the right to one. He lived a melancholy life in a world apart.
The death of our mother hours after giving birth to him had
bereft him of a breast to nurse on, and left him full of
questions without answers. The damage was much more
profound than we ever imagined. What happened later gave
us the measure, even though late, of the mortal wound
Bernardo received at birth. After my violent departure, my
father obliged him to take over the estate's accounts, and the
poor soul spent hours on end with columns of numbers that
never interested him. His true passion, if ever he had one
other than Dolores, remained hidden even from himself.

Cornelio Saavedra's letter was delivered to me on a

starless night, while I was completely lost in my writing. The pounding of a mysterious emissary who nearly knocked the door down marked the end of those happy dissolute years. I thought I was going to be told about my father's death, and I began to deny it, thinking of the guilt his passing without reconciliation would cause me. In all that time Francisco Rivas returned my correspondence unopened. It was his way of defeating me. I had started to write to him on the morning when I first discovered the gray while brushing my hair, and I decided that there was no longer any time or place for rancor. Bones continue to get weaker, and it is more and more difficult to hold them upright.

I remember that I read the letter the morning after receiving it, because my doubts would not permit me to go back to sleep, leaving me at the mercy of the night and its irreverence for my guilt. But that time I was wrong, so when I opened it, a cascade of events convulsing that far distant port city flooded my room. In his very long missive, my friend Saavedra urged me to return to Buenos Aires. Great changes were on the horizon, he told me, and he needed me by his side. He was feeling lonely and distrusted those who said they were his friends. He had been pressured into accepting the leadership of a conspiracy against Viceroy Cisneros and now, frightened by his boldness, he required my experience as a seasoned journalist in order to publish articles that would stir the city up, contradictorily submissive to England, but with libertarian ideas about Spain.

I needed no more excuses, and with the same impulse that years before had brought me to Lima, I set off on my inevitable road of return.

In spite of the friendships that were my support and of a handful of lovers who warmed my bed and my heart without asking too much, I always knew that I would not die in Lima. Even though I had twice been on the brink of marrying beautiful Limeñas, to this day I wonder why I left my brides crying over their dowry and their certain spinsterhood. I suppose that in the end I had a bit of conscience and reconsidered. If I could scarcely take charge of my own befuddlement, I was hardly going to be responsible for a fat wife like my father's and a raft of sniveling kids who resembled me.

Thus I left behind forever the place where I had awakened to conscience, where I learned on which side my own history was. Son of an Indian and a Spaniard like so many, I felt the tug-of-war between two bloodlines that would not accept mixing. But it was done. I was American and, as I had recently discovered, my writing had attained a degree of meaning and my heart had found peace.

Headed down the mountains toward Buenos Aires, I stopped in Tucumán and stayed just the length of time necessary to confirm that Francisco Rivas had not changed. He was old and sickly, but his animosity was still fresh.

To my surprise, Bernardo was the one who was totally transformed. He was hopelessly in love with a quiet girl the color of chestnuts who still played with dolls, and love made him glow.

She was Dolores Helguera, the daughter of a neighboring family, allied with ours by a casual proximity. I understood my poor brother Bernardo. Ignorant of feminine sweetness, that love, inflated by his imagination and neediness, transported him to places more gracious than reality. I did not wish to discourage him with warnings about the dangers hidden in all of that. He would discover them on his own. Today, as I write this memoir, I blame myself for leaving him alone with his heart.

Sitting with him in the gallery that looks out at Aconquija, in these mountains where even the air is joyous, I allowed myself to be tortured listening to his marriage plans, which did include the girl's growing up. He made these plans behind our father's back, since he was certain that he would not accept a marriage that did not signify an advantageous commercial transaction. Given Ignacio's desertion and mine, our father had exhausted his capacity for tolerance and was quite impatient to see the next generation of Rivases, knowing that neither of his estranged older sons, nor his chubby daughters, warranted spinsters, would give it to him.

Bernardo stumbled over himself trying to convey in words his belated happiness. I looked at him tenderly. He was over 30 years of age and had just recently opened his heart to a child of barely thirteen. I pleaded with him to make his dreams real without asking permission from life, and for the first time, I sensed that my brother was happy.

The morning of my departure when I embraced my father I realized that I would not see him alive again. Wrapped in a thick wool robe smelling of camphor, he had lost the ferocity that I remembered. I felt pity for us; life had slipped away as we inarticulately asked for help.

For the first time he let me embrace him. Even today I remember his hands on my back, clumsily stroking me in that belated encounter. But the problem with time is that it does not go backwards.

I arrived in Buenos Aires in June 1810, when the streets had not as yet been swept clean of the previous month's hopes and speculations for a peaceful revolution.

The city was strange to me after so many years of absence. It had stretched out in places that before had been impassable woods, and the streets were animated by an incessant racket. Public lighting reached to Montserrat Street, and there was no longer any need to put up barriers on rainy days to keep people from drowning in the reeking pot holes. What did remain the same was the plague of rats that moseyed about everywhere. Bigger than cats, one found them every two steps, disemboweled by happy hordes of children.

The obligatory place for meetings and political discussion was the Café de Marco, a modern eating establishment with billiard tables and an incredible array of alcoholic beverages. I began to get together again with my old work companions. Many were drowsing under the weight of a great belly and a prosperity gained through contraband. I felt quite distant from them. Luckily there were others, like Martín García who, like me, continued to search for his true place in life. As if you could recognize it the moment you found it, if that were ever to come about!

The wee hours found us drunk, full of fervor, and—mingled with a few sniffles—pledging eternal friendship, the violation of Princess Carlota Joaquina, and the death of the viceroy, although the last two could have been reversed.

Sometimes in the melee of wine and shifting of chairs by the bar's patrons, the poor blacks who came with little lanterns seeking their masters ended up taking the wrong one home, which much pleased some of the wives.

The month of May had disordered the lives of everyone and no one, not even the port authorities, knew what would happen with the Viceroyalty. They had exchanged the shame of being subjects of a dying Spain for the freedom to trade with France and England. Not much time passed for them to realize that they had arranged for the worst possible exchange of masters. But it was already too late.

Oh, Santa María de los Buenos Aires...!

What splendor! What a witches' Sabbath of colors, sounds, and aromas strolled through her poorly laid-out streets! In those times she proudly showed off her status as a capitol of the Viceroyalty and, in spite of that, how American she looked.

Buenos Aires was always cherished, from the very day she arose from the dreams of those crazed Spaniards who, after so many days of brine, founded her on the banks of a river.

All the vital juices that flowed together to engender her contended to leave their mark. Smiling black street-peddlers called out their wares, shaping themselves to the rhythm of their inner music. The irrepressible spark of Andalusia could be divined behind wrought-iron filigree and shawls that hid pretended modesties. Some of the lanterns illuminated French pretensions that in their finery reigned in the salons. Greedy English sailors looked at the riches that lounged about in the streets, slyly licking their lips. Absolutely everything was a whirlwind of vibrant life in that port city which as yet had no consciousness of its importance.

Buenos Aires had become accustomed to being the poor cousin of Mexico and Peru that, overflowing with gold and silver, tried to imitate European nobility. The first cry for independence would not come from them. It would be this untamed, solitary part of the continent that would be the first to put together a life not obligated to submission.

**Yemoja, mother of the fishes,
mother of the waters on Earth,
nourish me, Mother
protect and guide me, take away
the suffering I bear.
Grant me children,
don't let the witches devour me.**

*I sure did like to escape from the big house to go and skip
around in the streets! I buzzed about Missis like a bumblebee
and when somebody was needed to go out for an errand, I
was the first to volunteer. She always chose me because I
was smartest about the street and the one with the sharpest
wits of the five house servants who shared the heaviest work.
What I enjoyed the most was going to the beach and
stretching out on the sand to watch how they helped the
passengers down from those big boats and the sailors
shouting at the top of their lungs without anyone
understanding them. First they herded them down a little
ladder that hung over the side and moved around like a snake.
Then they sat them all quiet in boats tied to thick ropes that
some Percheron horses pulled on from the shore. That's how
they were brought in, jest using whips. And finally the sailors
put them in some narrow little canoes, and with the water up
to their waists, they pushed them like toys up to the shore.
And right there my eyes teared up from laughing to see them
soaked to the skin, with faces like they was important. The
women with lace parasols covered up their mouths when they
smelled the dead animals thrown on the beach or in the
puddles of brackish water. And I thought how different the
way we slaves got here from the way they did.*

*From standing there, mouth hanging open, it'd get so late
on me that I had to go running back to the house. Dirt got
stuck in between my toes, making my sandals so heavy that
every two steps I had to go back and look for them. I wasn't*

spared a knock on the head, but all the same I always managed things so I could go out the next day.

Truth is I always had my ways to work out every little thing. Whatever I got into my head, somehow or other, I got it done. From the time I was jest a young thing, my dream was to write my own name. All by myself I learned to write it.

From the inner patio, the one where they had the pots full of red begonias, you could hear the voices of the youngsters in the house, going over and over their abc's, repeating them, and while I swirled that month's soap in a big pot with a stick from the fig tree, like a parrot I'd imitate everything I heard. I didn't understand nothing, but I repeated it all. In the afternoon, when Missis and the children went out to call, I'd slowly go into the room, and with my hands real clean so as not to smudge, I'd shuffle through the pages that stayed on the table. There I'd stand quiet, staring at them for a long time, until each letter made the same sound as I'd recited in the patio. And you won't believe me, but one day I was able to write M A R I A. You recall that back in those days it was prohibited for us Negroes to learn to read and write.

One fellow, who lived close to the Plaza Mayor and learned jest by being pesky, got himself two hundred lashes. Me, knowing that, I wasn't going to be tricked, and I kept the secret good. When they sent me on an errand somewhere, I used to scrawl M A R I A with a stick in the driest part of the dirt in each block, to not forget it, of course. And later I'd rub it out with my foot. Don't you go believing I'm stupid.

When Sir Genrul began to be a little fond of me and found out about the hankering I had to learn, he made time and taught me my numbers so I'd know how to count. He told me I had a head for learning...

How could a body not feel tenderness for him seeing as how he was that way! Him I loved as much as my Mama. We were so close, Mama and me. The poor thing couldn't figure out who I took after, being so rebellious. She said maybe it was my granddaddy, who they killed over there in Africa when he went out to defend his family from the men that came in a big ship one day to bring them here like animals.

She told me all those stories when we'd finished in the kitchen, and it was a pleasure to sit together in the cool, all close and hugging, full of the smell of roses that came from the garden out back. You're not going to believe me, Mister, seeing me all old and poor, but over there in Africa my family was important, almost like kings. That was until those men with rifles I was telling about came and killed my granddaddy. Shoving them along, they loaded up the young in the village, and after a long voyage, they arrived here. But only the strongest made it. They say the others dropped dead from hunger and disease during the trip. I think those poor things died of sadness, fearing they'd never get back to their home. If you don't want to live, you are finally happy to die.

They jest went on throwing the dead ones overboard. Luckily, Yemoja took them down below, since she never abandons her children. My grandma and my Mama were lucky. The Marse bought them, and they was always treated good in the big house. But my grandma didn't withstand the grief and preferred to die. I understand her, you know. You call out for death when there's no room for you in life. And I assure you death never makes out she's deaf. At this moment that Nagó song I sang to put my little ones to sleep comes into my head. How did it start out ...?

My Augustín, my little boy! You're here with me tonight!

THREE

It was on that trip that their destinies became entangled

As soon as I arrived in Buenos Aires I found lodging two blocks from the Convent of San Francisco. The woman who owned the boarding house was a spinster who had met Ignacio on one of her trips to Italy and was still dazzled by his overacted saintliness. He always got good results when he rolled his eyes back and piously put his hands together.

On account of my being the brother of such an upright male, she did me the honor of renting me the only room that looked out on the street in that mansion. Its magnificent bedroom suite made of ebony inlaid with ivory made me feel affluent for the first time in my life, and the lascivious dreams I had in that imposing canopied bed to this day continue to be unconfessed. In order to make them more concrete, I received the priceless help of Barbara Estévez, a diminutive, youthful widow who lived across a street as narrow as her long-delayed desires were wide. In that way the great ebony bed lost its virginity at last, along with one or another little piece of ivory.

After years of absence, I embraced a husky, tight-lipped Saavedra, the highest authority in the Viceroyalty. I did not recognize him. Time had passed, but not enough to completely fray the image of that representative of Town Hall, who could ignite the people's applause with but a smile. Beaten down by a responsibility that was consuming him, he received me, making every effort to demonstrate the optimism he had lost. That night we dined, rushing our words and our food, trying to recount our lives to each other in an hour.

He confessed his anxiety while sharing a warm snifter of cognac in the well-stocked library of his home, while outside a persistent, silent rain fell, a sound I had forgotten in Lima.

"Gregorio, I regret the error of accepting the presidency of such a troublesome junta. They look at me with a lack of confidence, the fault of that traitor Moreno, who cannot wait to destroy me. But I too want to see him dead, though God may not forgive me."

The intellectuals in the group, led by Moreno, Castelli, and his cousin Belgrano, could not abide the fact that the common people, "smelling of the stable" as they put it, adored Saavedra so completely. They knew they could never inspire such love. And their hatred rested on that certainty.

That night of confessions and anxieties, he gave me the details of a plan that included me as an essential part. Every fifteen days, we would publish a thin gazette in which, entirely on my own, I would alert the people, especially the fervent young followers of Moreno, to the dangers of a change based on the violence which the little lawyer was so fond of.

Saavedra's idea was not bad. The written word was decisive in periods of change and until that moment in Buenos Aires, Moreno and Belgrano, both admirers of Europe, had had a monopoly on it, and thus had manipulated the opinions of young people.

I recall that I looked at him as he pensively evaluated his daring proposal, one I liked more and more. There I was, again returned to that city so hostile to me years ago. Had my hour of vengeance arrived? The volcano returned, and my hand began to move of its own accord. I would uncover the game of the Jacobins who had lined up behind Moreno, and I licked my chops thinking about how to annihilate them. Manuel Belgrano would go down with them, too timid to make his play out in the open. Words would continue to be what stitched my life together and that seemed good to me, very good. I doubted no longer and accepted the challenge.

Dawn broke while we were still finishing the details, which included organizing an opposition to neutralize the high-handedness of those clowns of the bullring who thought themselves to be the sole owners of the truth.

But my friend's idea had come too late. On a night of secrecy, out of Saavedra's earshot, in the midst of making sinister pacts, Moreno had conceived of a military expedition under the command of Manuel Belgrano. His mission consisted of convincing the timid inhabitants of Paraguay that they "ought" to imitate us and yield to the revolution in the port city, urgently breaking away from Spain.

The cornerstone of the politics of violence had been placed in what would forever be known as Buenos Aires' style.

The excellent reception the maneuver enjoyed exposed what little importance was given to the opinion of the president. Upon realizing his lack of authority, Saavedra sank into a state of apathy and terror, spending hours on end hidden away in his office, not wishing to see or to speak to anyone. Betrayal destroyed his vigor. He forgot about his journalistic plans, and I was left without knowing what in damnation I was doing in that city.

The guilt of not having utilized his authority as president in time began to eat away at him, and from his feverish ponderings came the idea that he communicated to me out of the blue one morning:

"Gregorio, you are the only one who can help me. Treachery surrounds me and I no longer know who is my friend or who will plunge a knife into me. I implore you to go with Manuel Belgrano and control his movements. Weapons will bring us no good, I can see that. Who the devil told me to get into this dance!"

In a desperate attempt to stop what he saw as the beginning of the end, the weakened Saavedra conceived of the crazy notion of sending me with the Expedition to Paraguay as something like a secretary, a combination scribe and spy. Under the pretext of making necessary official reports, I was to keep him up-to-date on all of Belgrano's movements.

At first I scornfully refused. I would not be a spy on my greatest enemy. I threatened and shouted at an increasingly more unshakeable Saavedra. I had not been summoned to debase myself in this way. And I continued shouting and threatening, but slowly the idea took shape in my mind. Perhaps the hour had arrived to avenge myself in a more concrete way than by means of some rag of a newspaper for the offenses my race suffered on account of so many like Belgrano, who now more than ever believed themselves to be the natural successors to Spanish power. Perhaps in this way, anticipating his clumsy movements, I could abort the Expedition and avoid the premature death of the new America we dreamed about in Lima...

No one obeys by chance, and for some reason I was in that place and in that circumstance. My moment had come and, without asking me for permission, my soul also got up on its feet. I vowed to become his shadow and anticipate his smallest decisions in order to inform my friends of whatever stupidity he dared to carry out. And I would have no pity at the moment I stopped him. As likewise he had had none for me when he humiliated me.

With the utmost secrecy, trustworthy people approached me every ten days, to take Saavedra the news of the activities of the lawyer recently anointed general.

"Do not hide or dissimulate anything, my friend. Only the truth of what is happening. Knowing the kind of man Belgrano is, I am sure he will invent his official reports."

When Belgrano learned that his old enemy was going with him, he went red in the face as he had before. They say that the tantrum he threw was huge.

As superior as always, he continued to believe that there was no authority greater than his. But he was wrong. In a final attempt to recoup his lost dignity, Saavedra yelled louder and pounded his desk with his fist, and the next day my name was extensively noted in the orders for the Expedition *they're presenting me with your head on a silver platter oh when I do fall on you worthless little doctor of laws now I am bound to you by my writing I have to hide that I'm a journalist to become your nanny but you're going to pay up I'm not going to let you breathe easy I'm going to get into your thoughts under your skin oh you stupid little Goldilocks your nightmare is just beginning and you don't even suspect a thing...*

It was on that journey that our three destinies began to be entangled, only to be untangled by death. In the name of hate or love, María, he, and I were united beyond what we would have ever wished. We learned late that the price of excess is death and destruction.

What had been rounded up to go to Paraguay was deserving of many names, but never the name of "Army." It was a bunch of poor, disoriented human beings. The majority were blacks and mulattoes who were fleeing from hunger in search of a daily meal. The rest were boys who had scarcely begun to shave and militiamen still warm from the fires of the English invasion. But the racket they made was contagious and they had life on their side. Barefoot and ragged, they considered themselves soldiers of Napoleon. They were so happy and confident of victory that I felt that contradicting them was a sin.

The last thing I learned before leaving was that Ignacio announced his definitive domicile was Vatican City and he had no thought of returning from there for the next fifty years. Poor, weak Bernardo carried on, subjected to the will of my father who tried to force him to be the man he could never be. I also received a happy letter in which he told me of incredible progress in his relationship with Dolores Helguera. Apparently, our father was softened by the proximity of death and the fear that the Rivas name would disappear under the weight of his fat daughters. And one unexpected afternoon, he took off his robe, covered the odor of camphor with flower water, and for the last time put on his brown velvet suit, his fine linen shirt and, leaning on Bernardo's arm, headed for the neighboring house of the Helgueras to ask officially for Dolores' hand. Of course it was conceded immediately since the Rivas' wealth was an excellent motive to drink to the felicity of the engaged couple. The agreement, and my brother's luck, were sealed forever in a champagne toast in the main dining hall of the girl-bride's home. In that way, Bernardo began to travel the road that led him toward becoming the most unhappy being I have ever known. He had no defenses against Dolores' evil love that years later would tear him apart.

Today I believe that what I did was sufficient. I know that nothing will return my brother to me. But vengeance helps one to go on, by alleviating the burden of life.

I am certain that, had Bernardo known that I annihilated the man who was killing him while he was still alive, something like a smile would have adorned his mouth. Even though he had stopped smiling quite a while ago.

How gods and men do get mixed up together!

The inhabitants of El Tambor had the rare ability to forge the customs brought from their land with those that the dominant religion in the new territory–where they arrived enslaved–wished to impose on them.

Proud of their ancestral rites and customs, they had made their Olympus Creole enough and, with intuitive selectivity, had taken from the Church only that which was harmonious with the family of gods most proximate to them.

The vibrant cacophony of African tongues that the elders spoke as a final rebellion against their destiny spread out under the sun everyday.

Children and grandchildren respectfully spoke them in the presence of their elders. But out of their hearing and amongst themselves, they spoke a Creole that was gestating, whose edges they blurred in order to inject their Nagó, Congo, and Bantú words. It was the new language of this land that, without knowing it, they would mark definitively.

Whoever passed through the barrio and had vision beyond the surface of things could see Okó singing into Juan's brown ear as he braided Guinea corn into brooms, and the wise Erinle beside the witch doctor guiding his hand as he cured a sick man, or see Orishás in a mirror held up by an adolescent bursting with sensuality, telling her about the oldest tricks of seduction. Gods and men, disdaining the earthbound realm, lived there and helped others to live.

For the festivals of San Benito, all the inhabitants of El Tambor, San Telmo, and Montserrat were convened out of love for their patron and came out into the main thoroughfares of the city in a colorful, musical parade. And such was their devotion to the saint, where some saw the face of Olorúm and others Obatalá, that they made the city slow its pace to watch him pass by, enveloped in the music of mazacayas and the rhythmic couplets of his devout followers.

Oggún, make me strong. Oggún, the powerful. The Strong One of the earth. The Great One from the other world. The Protector of the suffering. Oggún, give me strength.

Like I was telling you, there came a morning when my mama couldn't get out of her cot. I'd been noticing her a mite slow grinding the grains of corn, she could hardly lift the pestle and she wouldn't let me help her, simply out of pride.

That day I left her lying down and made her take a little tea of goat's rue with valerian, to treat lack of gumption. But in the afternoon she got a fever and she couldn't even open her eyes from being so feeble. Saying her prayers, she got even worse. Right then and there I got scared and went to ask the Marses for help. They sent me to look for Don Ricardo, their own doctor. I know we were slaves, but they always treated us like family. The doctor was crazy about the vizcacha empanadas we made on Sundays. I made bunches of them the Christmas I spent at the North with the soldier boys, don't ask me how many. From crimping the edges, my hand stayed all cramped up for three days, and that was with a few courteous but pretty lazy helpers. Still, with all the hunger there was, you can't imagine the effort they made. After they ate them, I recall that they even gave me a round of applause. Up there that really was a banquet, after spending days and days with only jerky.

Well, I'll continue. What's happening is that I'm going 'round in circles, I don't want to remember so clearly. Don Ricardo told me it was a matter of waiting, and he gave her a brown liquid. But my heart was telling me that we couldn't wait, that she was dying on me. And dark night already fallen, right then and there, I wrapped her up in a blanket and, as they told me she'd done with me when I was born, with two chambermaids we carried her bodily to Mama Basilia's place. The instant she saw us arrive, she put her down on a cot and commenced to invoke Ori and the Virgen del Rosario. She prepared her a tea with Oggún's ewes, by mixing eucalyptus, alfalfa, parsley, bloodroot, and cacao. Me, I prayed to the Virgin, who always granted me things, but real soft so the Orishás couldn't hear me. But that night it must have been that she was busy because my mama died anyway.

I wasn't able to be convinced, I swear. I even lay down right up close to her so I could give her the warmth of my body and I sang her Nagó songs. To wake her up, I was thinking. What a fool, eh? How could she leave me all alone! We'd been such buddies! Who was going to give me her blessing and then tell me, "Sweetie, you my treasure."?

And say, you know, isn't that it? That's the way things are. Nobody ever beat death. You can just barely slow it down with spells, but sooner or later it comes. How well I learned that with the Tucuman.

Next morning real early the Marses showed up, carrying a coffin in the big carriage to take her to the church buryingground. And what can I say? When I saw him standing there, avoiding my eyes and frightened with so much death, my hunch came back to me. Yah, don't laugh. I had takings since I was a little girl. Chosen of the gods, that's what Mama Basilia said I was. That's why those hunches came to me like dreams, and sometimes like a racing of my heart or a lightning bolt that lit me up and made me fall down to my knees. But here's the thing, they never let me down. So many times I would've wished to be wrong. A hunch that came to me was a hunch that came to pass.

All right, I was telling you that when I saw the Marses that day, the certainty came too that he was my papa; it couldn't be anybody else. How had I been so blind the whole time? It's probably a sin, but I got mad, really mad, that I had his blood and from him nothing, ever. Nary a sign so's I might reckon why I was lighter than the other slaves. My mama surely must have suffered with the weight of such a secret! And right then and there on the spot I asked him to go back from where he'd come from, that my mama we were going to bury as a Yoruba, as what she was. I think he realized I'd discovered the secret. It was most likely on account of that he went away all silent, without looking at me. It wore on me later, to become accustomed to my white part, but what was I to do? The blood was already mixed together.

About the funeral, what I most recall are the songs and drums that didn't stop that entire day, and they kept on all the way to the cemetery. Up ahead went the box drum played by young men from the Nagó nation. Between Mama Basilia and the Babalawo from San Telmo, I went behind, wearing a dress that Miss Eloisa had made me a present of, blue and black, so elegant. The rest came along, at times dancing and at times weeping. We loved my poor little dead mama so much that it pained us to leave her so alone in the burying ground. At each corner we would stop to rest and dry the perspiration from all the hustling about. The boys left the coffin on the two chairs brought by Luis, the Cisneros' mulatto, and the dancers going at it, 'round the coffin to please Olorúm and ask him to take my mama with all the Orishás, to rest after so much fatigue.

And I never returned to the big house. For what? From there I went to live with Mama Basilia who needed me for her conjuring. The poor soul was getting so old and blind that she confused the stones for divining.

I might have been ungrateful, but after learning who the Marses was for real, I couldn't go back. Now as an old woman, I realize I always knew it without knowing it. The truth was so big it'd become invisible.

FOUR

Nothing can resemble that inferno

From the first time I saw her coming into camp ready to go to Paraguay, around September 1810, I knew that I would have no peace until I saw her without her colorful clothing, dressed only in her hot chocolate-colored skin.

And that's how it was. The opportunity came about later than my galloping desire wanted, but it came.

In those days just before setting off, while Belgrano was in charge of the final preparations of the improvised army, she came into our lives, never to leave again.

It was a morning lit by the sun and dreams. The whole camp held still, watching. Tall, upright, wrapped in the rainbow of her clothes, with a slender waist and breasts the essence of firmness, she was a true apparition. Her sure confidence allowed no one to stand in her way, not even to ask her what she was doing there. Making her way past immobile tools, weapons, and soldiers, she did not even bother to notice, she looked around for the general until she found him delivering orders to a group of officers. With a determined tread, amidst that whirlwind of veils and necklaces, she came to a stop in front of him, giving him a salute, part reverence, part standing at attention so comically serious that I had no choice but to adore her from that moment on.

"Good mornin', your Excellency, I'm going with you. The officers and Sir Genrul need somebody to wash and iron for 'em. Uh, and I can use a rifle too!"

More than asking him permission, she was announcing to him that she would come along with us, whether he liked it or not.

"There is no place for women, much less so if they are

Negroes," said Belgrano's deprecating silence and furrowed brow.

Indifferent to his hardened stance she continued with her discourse: "Sir, the Junta is asking for help for you all. In the *Gaceta* it says that women are giving up their gold. I'm offering my work, sir. I'm not lazy and I killed a passel of English."

He looked without a word and, turning his back on her as if he had neither heard nor seen anyone, continued giving his orders. I never found out if she took that gesture as a mute acceptance or if she did not care a whit for his disdain, because she left a pile of her things close to a tree, rolled up the sleeves of her blouse, and went straight to stick her head in an enormous black pot from which only delicious morsels came from that moment on.

The next day I sidled up to her jokingly serious and gave her a canvas bag to put her things in. With eyes full of laughter, but very serious in mute complicity, she filled it to the top with a clean, threadbare blanket, two bunches of clothing, four cakes of soap that she confessed she had made for the occasion, a maté tea, a hen turkey, and a flat-iron made of steel that more than once I saw crash down on a Barbarian's head.

I never understood what made him accept her, given the unlimited disparagement he felt for Negroes. I can only attribute it to the fact that, beyond his will, the three of us were supposed to travel together during those years so that things would happen as was written. That is, if stories of love and death are written down somewhere.

Her hot mouth made me lose my sense of being ridiculous, and I was simply a pathetic forty-year-old inhabited by a young man in heat. María or Kumbá, she had the name of my desire. I had waited all my life for the woman who had the answers I lacked, and it only took one look to discover that she had brought them with her.

In their loneliness, over time the boys baptized her

"Auntie María," and whoever does not remember her cannot say that he was with Manuel Belgrano on his military campaigns to Paraguay and Upper Peru. To my despair, and, revenge piled on revenge, she was his faithful shadow and loved him beyond his death.

"We were born on the same day," she boasted, wanting to encounter in that coincidence, impossible to verify, the motive for the strange relationship that united them from the day they met.

I close my eyes and I can still see her in the camp, at night beside the embers where she heated her iron, with the habitual pipe in her mouth, ironing Manuel Belgrano's clothes with sure movements. So when he awoke in the imprecise light of dawn, drenched by malignant fevers, his uniform ironed and mended, a sparkling white shirt awaited him at the foot of his cot. One could doubt that the sun would come up, but never that his clothing would be in its place.

Why deny it now, if time passing took charge of smoothing the edges of my pride, jealousy choked me when I verified the ties that bound them and left me out in the cold.

Some time later he discovered at last the exact place to strike me when one night he encountered me covered with her scent after I'd left her. On the pretext of dictating urgent correspondence, he had my cot placed beside his, and he would awaken me in the middle of the night to dictate ludicrous reports that the next day, smiling defiantly, he would tear up in my face. He expected a reaction like the ones from our time at the Colegio de San Carlos. But I never again gave him that pleasure. This time he would not control my life.

On other occasions, I was the one who woke myself up at some ungodly hour, and watching him sleep so defenseless, imagined how easy it would be to make him slip from sleep into death. With his very poor health, who would suspect me? In point of fact, I suspected myself. The time I spent watching him sleep was excessive.

My mulatto conquered even the most hardened soldiers with her irreverent sympathy, curing them of problems with bones, homesickness, and the hard lessons of time.

The young men came to her seeking consolation, Nagó herbs and songs, and for those of her race, she was another one of their gods in a crowded Parnassus. And so I needed to elbow myself into a place in her life among the many followers.

How could I have gone crazy for an old mulatto was a question I heard too many times. I never lacked for women with inviting looks and there was no skirt I wanted that my hands wouldn't pull down without delay. No one who did not know her as I did can understand it. It was not merely the aroma of her proud female person that trapped me. It was that unconquerable tender fiber, that soft ferocity that she carried in her heart and in her lap that bound me to her almost to asphyxiation. The female she was bound me to her skin, and the woman she was bound me to her soul.

Only someone who has been on a battlefield, where one encounters death face to face, holding a weapon you dare not fire, where your foot slips in pools of enemy blood all churned up together, can understand me. At that exact point where life and death fall in love, there, you can understand how indispensable a woman's hand is that closes the eyes of the dead, that covers the wounds of the living, that touches us and softly absolves those of us who kill for the first time. And that was what she was always there for.

I remember her; I live for that: seeing her steep maté for me to the point of perfection, and listening attentively to me pluck the petals of my love all mixed up with failures and discouragements, in that gesture of human understanding so much her own. Or committing herself to reconstruct my uniform's lost dignity with needle and thread, consoling me so the jealousy that from then on never again left me would not hurt so much *desire desire desire how good it is to smell you to touch you my little mulatto my negrita how is it you don't realize he hates you he doesn't love you he doesn't desire you he doesn't burn he doesn't smell you as I do what sweet eyes you have negrita how fast your hands negrita how would a caress of yours be I don't know why we are going to the Paraguay River but we are going together what luck it's so hot I cannot stand this shitty uniform but you will be my reward pretty negrita the sweat gets into my eyes and they burn this is how I'll sweat when I have you you sweat with the smell of a female in heat it drives us all crazy but not him my little mulatto you don't drive him mad pretty negrita nothing gets him aroused I don't know what he takes pleasure in well yes I do know what he likes but even so I never saw him happy.*

And so it was that September 1810, with no scent of orange blossoms, that we of the first Military Expedition, left Buenos Aires.

I screwed up my courage, put on the coarse blue uniform, loaded up a book of folio pages, a briefcase with sheets for correspondence, my inkwell and a collection of pens, and disconcertingly, with my heart beating with contradictions and certainties, joined up with that column of ragged soldiers who, like me, squeezed the trigger with their eyes closed and went off happily in a direction that was as uncertain as luck.

From the first day that the sloppy columns of men began to march and through that entire journey, with the art of fencers, he and I avoided contact of any kind. But if, by accident, we came together in some place, we bristled, ready for the attack. I had had enough of his nights and his whims.

When my need to suffer his arrogance choked me to the point of vomiting, I would burst into the meetings he conducted with his officers. Making the face of an idiot and using the voice of one, I begged him to edit the reports to Buenos Aires that I had left purposely incomplete the night before. A transformation took place on the spot, and barely containing his wrath, he answered, "Warnes will take care of it, Rivas. Leave it. Dismissed." Then, seeing him flushed as in the past, I went away satisfied.

I perceived that in that one-upmanship the winner would be the one who withstood the longest. But I had the advantage of remembering the weight of injustice. From childhood on, I was accustomed to my father who, in the face of my disobedience, punished me by locking me up in the pantry with the bushels of flour, tallow candles, and frying pans, hoping a repentant son would emerge from there. He never succeeded. Opening the door, he invariably encountered a furious demon who confronted him. I never changed.

The nightmare we lived through during that expedition continues to wake me in the middle of the night. Surrounded by diabolical flora, our journey under that lethal sun presented a test many of us did not pass. The heat and the insects pitilessly besieged us and not even having been born in a climate like Tucumán's served me well. Nothing can resemble that inferno. The insect bites became infected to such an extent that soon we were covered with enormous pustules that the uniform's thick fabric made into active volcanoes constantly erupting.

As we moved deeper into that green inferno, that asphyxiating purgatory, María became more necessary than the expedition's two doctors. They were paralyzed by so much book learning that they contemplated but could not forestall death caused by those tropical diseases not described in the books of medicine they had brought from Europe. After being at first openly hostile to the mulatto and disdainful of her remedies, when they were faced with a reality that superseded their strength and knowledge, they became a harmonious team of science and spells together.

Her poultices and plasters were truly miraculous, and even the most diehard skeptic surrendered before the evidence of their effectiveness when he saw a sick man, at nightfall the captive of very high fevers, get up full of energy the next day; or feel the immediate relief on feet torn up from so many days of marching by her applying a preparation of yarrow, olive oil, and cane liquor in equal parts. It was a recipe she gave in to distributing to all, and in the face of its enormous success she didn't have enough to go around.

But, in spite of all her spells, when the city gates from which we had departed were simply a distant, dried-up memory for the storytellers, all those who had forgotten they were human beings began to die like flies, victims of dysentery and hemorrhaging that finally triumphed over María. Thirst cracked us open all the way to our souls and we drank rotten, stinking water to moisten our parched, scabby lips. Throughout the whole march, we withstood downpours so violent that when they let up, men, animals, and belongings were covered in a sticky red mud that made impossible any movement of our bodies or our spirit. After those rains, the sun would mercilessly appear in a cloudless sky, making steam thicker than fog.

And as if all those tricks of nature were insufficient, one night we discovered the mortal danger of the carachás monkeys. Wild monkeys, bigger than a man, they seemed to have escaped from the alcoholic nightmares of my past. And, in spite of the fact that the night guard was reinforced, they dedicated themselves to dining on the guards, whom we would find in the first light of morning, torn apart, their pieces scattered.

Immune to any inconvenience, María slipped through the camp like a princess overseeing her subjects. And I was always following her. Trapped as only a crazy man can be by a passion so huge that it forgave hers for my enemy, I sought the moment to undress her and make mine that body I desired so feverishly. Wanting her was, at that moment, more seductive than having her. My overheated imagination did not want to ask permission; it needed to come to her body, trembling with the fear of being discovered. Obsessed, waiting for the moment, I was convinced that when we might make love, one of us would have to die with the terrible force of our surrender. And I pleaded that it be me.

I push my memory trying to recall when she became indispensable. It is not easy. To recall does not reside in the memory but rather in the heart. Perhaps it was when I first heard her sing in Nagó, invoking her gods. Every sundown she withdrew out of sight. I secretly followed, unable to resist the pleasure of spying on her. She kneeled, looking to the west, and she slowly placed tureens with fruits, water, and colored stones down in front of her. She remained still for a time, a brown statue, and then began her plaintive, unintelligible chant, with which she called to her gods. A group of Negroes who remained respectfully kneeling at a certain distance from their priestess always accompanied her. Their voices moaned with a nostalgic, monotone melody that tore your heart apart. She rocked softly with her eyes closed, far beyond the here and now. Her voice arose clear, calling for heaven's pity, and the chorus of blacks answered, accompanying themselves with hand claps in a precise, sacramental sound. I swear to this day that the magic could be touched and that the gods came to visit her. Regardless of the time elapsed since then, whenever I encounter an anguished twilight, those sounds of invocation ring in my ears.

Manuel Belgrano's old obsession with order and organization turned out to be as tiresome as it was useless. He clung to ridiculous patterns, intuiting that he was gambling his prestige on the success of his mission. Sitting whole nights long in the light of a lantern before his maps of the area, he chose the best route, and changed it the next day, furious because he was now dealing with a swollen river that had to be forded, or an impassible road that required a detour. It was an effort for him to learn that nature never had a directive from an embassy and that life does not provide maps of routes marking shortcuts for suffering, and that the cost of his apprenticeship should be paid by the humblest ones.

One February During Carnival
Love Sought You Out

Excitement grew in the barrio of El Tambor as Carnival approached. Women obliged their needles to hurry the costume-making, and the colors of those fancy clothes contended together in a war without winners. Over and over the dancers repeated their frenetic movements to the sound of marimbas and mazacayas that like tyrants commanded repetition to the point of perfection of those dance steps not in time with their mandate:

> aié -hé – hé
> hé – hé – hé
> samba catamba – yé

Vibrant voices melded together with the drums, and a magic, sensual climate was born, which even the whites didn't draw back from, darkening their skin to mix with the blacks, the exclusive proprietors of the festival.

Anyone who looked at María was moved by an enormous temptation to fall down at her feet. How majestic she appeared, upright and proud, in her dress made from a rainbow! Placed behind the elders who headed the procession, she seemed to be a queen in whose honor this whole unfolding of life, music, and color was being carried out.

The noisy shot fired from the fort signaled permission for the gaiety of Carnival to overflow from San Telmo, El Tambor, from Mondongo, and all the black barrios opened their veins so their music and their blood would move through the city, bathing it year after year in the repeating ritual.

From that point on for three days, the great village exiled its serene salons, and a lack of restraint took ownership of the streets and plazas, to the futile horror of the clergy. Because once set loose, Carnival was no longer the patrimony of blacks; it became the frenzy of the scantily-clad girls of good families. They played with water in the company of ardent cousins who stopped the running girls with the aid of the remotest dark corners of the house.

Night and day, the hypnotic rhythm of the drums transported those who let themselves be possessed by its cadences.

The drums beat as if bewitched, their rhythm, making love to cencerros and adjás, penetrated through the feet of the dancers, inhabiting the entire body, and took possession triumphantly. So, frenzied and bathed in sweat, men and women became confused together, woven in and out, they mixed, converged, and flowed together in zarabandas, ombligadas, and chikás that foretold the passion that, under the cloak of shadows, would hours later make riot in all sorts of blood.

Anyone who saw Kumbá dance could never forget her. Her body was the fantasy that helped many to await their freedom at next year's Carnival. She began to move slowly, very slowly. With her hips making unbelievable angles, her cadenced rhythm brought the frenzied beating of the instruments to a stop. She made the sounds linger at her waist and trapped the song in the smooth waving of her arms. And for a magical instant, the blacks forgot the Carnival around them and, torn away, they returned to the continent from which they'd been uprooted. Because then she was no longer Kumbá, but became Yemoja, the sea mother of so many orphans she consoled with the belated rocking of her cradle.

How necessary she was for all of them, Kumbá from Buenos Aires, María Nagó! How necessary as well for the nation!

And turning the corner, running barefoot and happy so the flying eggshells filled with colored water that in Carnival streaked the skies of the barrio didn't reach her, she ran

44

into him, the other one. Black Manuel grasped her by the shoulders, and when he moved her aside to continue on his way, she recognized him. He was her life's companion, the man she'd have children with. He tried to be on his way again, ignorant of the prophecy, but Kumbá, with a knowing excuse, stopped him and made him look at her. And he was forever bound to her eyes.

**You should realize that obstinacy
does not benefit anyone; that the truth
told to us has to be paid attention to.
(One of the sixteen Moral Rules of the Odu)**

*So, youngster, are you going to remain standing there?
C'mon, c'mon, take a seat. Don't worry...*

*My, it's hot tonight! Thanks to the Virgin this hammock is
so comfortable that, by supporting my back good, I almost
don't feel any pains. Why, getting old has been something
fierce! The worst is you don't realize how quickly the years
pass by, and one day you tell the body to do something it has
always done and the shameless ol' thing gets moody. But I
still have my ways and I ease the pains with my poultices. Be
it with swinecress, quinine seed, ginseng, or China root,
depending on what hurts. Folks still coming to see me so I
can cure them, and I jest do it.*

*I learned so much from Mama Basilia. Jest as soon as
she took me to live with her she taught me all the secrets of
curing, of talking with the Orishás, of divining the future. By
and by I became an Iyalorishá. When I was born I had
already gotten the protection of the warrior Orishás against
evil, which even though nobody believes it, is closer to human
peoples than what you might imagine.*

*In time and though I didn't find any fun in it, she kept on
teaching me how to throw the divining stones so as to read
the future. I say what's the need! The only thing it's good for
is making bad blood before its time. I didn't want to learn
much about all that. It was only to please Mama Basilia. A
body suffers a lot knowing what's coming up. It happened to
me. For many years I saw Sir Genrul in my dreams, always
jest surrounded by bad omens. And so, from the time he first
appeared in person, I suffered every day waiting for those
things to come to pass. And look, see if they didn't.*

*After the battles of Salta and Tucumán came the
slaughterhouses of Vilcapugio and Ayohuma. So much young*

blood. What a useless way to die! Some didn't even have whiskers. I cried for them, but I cried more for their mothers, since losing a son is as though they'd yanked life out of a mother without killing her.

Don't you go fooling yourself, young man. I may have loved Goldilocks, but I didn't let him get by with things so badly done as Ayohuma. Right then and there he had to listen to me. I told him everything I had swallowed for so long. To be so mule-headed to have his own way, being deaf and prideful when any ol' dumb thing was brought up to him, and what poisoned me the most was the shabby way he always treated people of my race. You could see his disgust when he gave orders to the Black and Browns. For him, everything we did was bad; we were lazy, tricksters, had loads of gods when there was only One. My Sir Genrul never believed in my gods. What are you going to do? That's how he was.

The one who sure did believe in Shangó was the Tucuman. He passed the time with his papers, waiting for the moment to grab me alone. When I least expected it, he'd come up from behind, hug me, and begin to put his hands all over me, so sometimes he'd get a slap. He came after me so intently that in the end he found me real good.

After my black Manuel died, I went to bed many times with the desire for a man. Yah, don't laugh, boy. The years don't frighten off a body's desires. They make 'em stronger. And when the occasion presents itself, you enjoy it more than when you was younger because you don't know if it'll be the last time or not.

Ayohuma… I remember as if it had been yesterday how all the Barbarians slid down from out of those hills. They came with the smell of death on them. Shangó made me smell it, and when I tried to warn Sir Genrul, he paid me no mind at all. He was attending the mass that he made the priest who was with us say. All of that for nothing. His god yawned in his face. And of course, while we were crossing ourselves, marking our bodies with crosses, those others, comfy as you please, surrounding us on all sides, and they came down on us.

Why my Sir Genrul was real good-looking! It was a pleasure to see him up on a horse, wearing his blue broadcloth uniform with nary a stain on it. That's what I took charge of, and I don't have to make out being modest as I always had it spotless for him. Straight and stiff as a rod, the poor soul looked around with eyes that seemed to be seeing things that only he knew about, and that's why they were kind of droopy sad. Anybody who didn't know him thought he was the picture of health walking around at all hours without a pause. But I sure did have to help him through the nights. When I felt some scared soldier boy shaking me, I leaped up, and stumbling in the darkness, went to his tent. I already knew why they were looking for me. I went in and there the poor soul was, soaking with sweat, clothes plastered to his body. At times he was crazy and called out for people I didn't know. When that happened I made them all leave quiet and I'd take these magical charms out of this bag that I still have here tied to my waist that Mama Basilia gave me before she died.

I put them on the ground and soft, soft so nobody would hear me I began to chant, calling for Ifá to cure my Sir Genrul. If he didn't hear me, I called San Benito, so together they'd try harder and carry away that malignant fever. And he jest took it away. I tell you even that doctor, who looked at me sideways at first, later on called for me hush-hush. I seized the opportunity, and when he was sleeping and started to breathe steady, I would give him a big bear hug, and I'd cover him with kisses that jest came out, and I'd real soft say to him things that not even if I was out of my mind would I repeat. Things of my own. And don't look at me that way so's I'll tell you neither. If something happened between us, that's my thing too. Not you or anybody has a need to know that his scent still comes to me while I'm sleeping.

You can't even imagine what I felt for my Sir Genrul.

That's why at times like tonight when I recall what Tucuman did to him, guilt wants to get into me. I don't let it. I only jest figured it out in the end, when the damage was already done.

Tonight I have a hunch I'm not alone, and it's not an old woman's foolishness. I close my eyes and see all the faces of my deceased. How many there are! They're smiling and it's as if they wanted to say something to me. It ought to be something pretty because they look contented. If they could talk to me... You who's younger, can't you hear if they're calling me?

FIVE

How tiresome I was for fair Manuel Belgrano in Paraguay!

After almost a month of marching, everything was cause for argument between the two of us. At that point he already had real doubts about my true mission. Attempting to catch me he would set ridiculous traps that I dodged with no less ridiculous explanations. Though he might not like it, I was put there by the President of the Junta and no one could change that. I was happy when I saw his hatred throbbing in the vein in his forehead that was oh so pale it made even his emotions transparent.

So I enjoyed an ambiguous status, between being a uniformed scribe and a public spy, and I took advantage of it to not remain under orders that were intended to break me.

The general officer's staff had no reasons for hating me. In fact we got along well from the first day. They were not much different from my idealist friends in Lima and we even gathered to get drunk on the sly several nights, thus forgetting for a few hours where life had put us. But since they owed the commander their loyalty, out of obligation they directed at me a lazy, distracted ill-will. The heat did not allow them to take responsibility for other people's passions.

In spite of knowing that my letters were anxiously awaited in Buenos Aires, it daily became more difficult to comply with my task as informant. Where to put my annoyance at being in a strange place while not betraying my pact with Saavedra? The expedition was delirious and nonsensical. Most of the troops appeared to be on a trip to the country rather than on a march to war, and the Negroes went along barefoot and happy to feel free. They did not have the slightest idea of the war effort's objectives, but they did not care too much to know what they were, either. And it was much better that way.

Knowing my weakness for maté, the mulatto offered me a nice bitter one whenever she could. She would approach me smiling, unaware of the pounding in my veins, and I bubbled over with her sensual smell that I hungrily breathed in. The desperation to make her mine ended up disarticulating my body and soul. I stopped paying attention to the reports that I was to put together every two days and, thanks to my overheated state, Saavedra had no reports from me. I could not wait any longer. The moment had to come. And it did.

It was a very early morning with a moon so bright that it transformed María into a silvery statue. I came upon her, thinking she was not able to be seen, as she slithered down in the nearby arroyo in search of water's cool relief. She believed that at that hour no one would notice her absence, but waiting for my opportunity I followed her, tracking her every movement like an animal in heat. I waited for her to move further into the darkness, putting a distance between herself and the camp with its vigilant eyes.

I stopped her before she got to the shore, taking her by the shoulders from behind. I turned her around with the urgency of centuries and kissed her on the mouth. She was not surprised, and pressing herself against my body, held me with the same force as I held her. We hugged each other for the first time in the world, one we had too long awaited. We dropped down in a mêlée of clothes torn off, kissing, wrapping ourselves up together, blurring the contours of each body until we were forged into only one, in the pure pleasure of that anticipated spasm, unforeseen, fleeting, eternal. Biting each other, sucking each other. She closed her eyes and I licked the chocolate of her skin like a tame dog. Naked, satiated the first time, waiting for the second, two times, two deaths, two lives.

The hunt had been interesting. But after that full moon, I preferred the sin. We said our goodbyes in that period between the last stars and the first rays of the sun. In silence we erased the other's telltale traces that stayed in our clothes that stuck to us from the humidity of our bodies and the dirt. We sensed that words would deflate the moment and destroy the magic full of certainties that we had lived.

In spite of the pain in my bones and muscles, un-accustomed to love's violence, I returned to my obligations with more energy than ever. But there were things that not even our surrender that night could change. I well knew that I was not the only object of her preoccupations. Aware of Belgrano's fragile health, María had brought him under her fierce tutelage, ignoring his gestures of irritation. She devoutly prepared him what little food he put in his mouth, and the looks of adoration that she directed his way were so obvious, and she sought with such zeal to be close to him, that soon her idolatry was the motive for whispered joking and there did not lack for a daring soul who, one night, strummed a guitar that whispered:

> Oh, María, who'd wonder
> how much you love Manuel.
> Would you dare one day or other
> to make that known to him as well?

I also had to become accustomed to a somber, ponderous jealousy, and had no recourse but to hide a passion that perhaps for being well-guarded lived until the end.

There were such adversities in each day's marching that only spirits tested by fire remained immune, and Maria's was one of those. She had a uncanny knack for improvisation. If the camp's stores were scarce, she hovered over the huge pots and presented us with a undeniably flavorful meal of uncertain origin. If the cowhide we made our boats with was stretched too tight and split, she wet it again and rubbed it with a paste of her own invention that miraculously sealed the torn edges. She did not allow the tricks of life to defeat her.

At that point in the march a bad mood that flared up at the slightest vexation had overpowered me. I cursed myself for having accepted Saavedra's proposal, and I could no longer find any meaning in my mission. Belgrano joined me in the foul mood that in him grew when he had to deal with the military inefficiency of the officers who accompanied him. In one of his attacks of impotence against a reality that overcame him, I was his victim: "Rivas, people with idle hands are not needed here. From now on, you will take charge of inventorying all the weapons and ammunition we need. Send letters to God and the Most Holy Mary. You like to write so much, take this opportunity..."

Despite his intention to rile me up, that order snapped me out of the inertia and lethargy I found myself in, and I turned to the classification and accounting of the ordinance, with the help of an old mulatto, a militiaman during the British Invasions, who conveyed to me the secrets of those tools destined to kill. I became an expert in artillery ammunition. I learned to distinguish between rifle bullets, musket balls, flintstones. I discovered the necessity of relying on mortars, their swabs and buckets of grapeshot, with carriages in good shape to move the cannons singly or in pairs. I kept primers, fuses, and ramrods with wads in perfect condition. I learned how to check the condition and sharpness of bayonets, lances, sabers, and swords. And I confess, to my surprise, that I became enamored of that concrete, lethal world. The only thing that truly justified my uniform, on the edges of the inferno that scorched inside and outside, was her proximity and the promise of nights and their moons

Not until we had the majestic Paraná before us could we imagine the difficulties that awaited us in crossing that enormous, almost oceanic, extent of brown, churning water. After the extenuating march, not a soul resisted the temptation to bathe in it. Some were expert fishermen and, guided by a group of Guaraní Indians who approached with childlike surprise, they made harpoons from lances and attached ropes, and pulled out dorados and catfish in a quantity so large that, as in the biblical multiplication, the feast was for all.

Cannons, firearms, batteries, foodstuffs, ammunition, and the rest of the equipment, already deteriorated by age and abuse, was the huge cargo that was supposed to arrive safely on the other shore, all of it, not counting the other goods of a spiritual nature that the chaplain who accompanied us dragged along for the care of our souls.

With the aid of the Indians and scouts, the troop improvised rafts of hide and wood with which we crossed the water. Some of the crafts did not make it to the other shore, and there they still lie on the bottom of the river, orphans without explanations, belongings that were never displayed. Those who did get there, after having suffered from the unruly waves, deposited the wet firearms and the moist, useless powder on the sand.

The night before the battle, while I was with the officers gathered to finalize the details that multiplied at every turn, María came up to me terrified and, falling to her knees at my feet, screamed: "The bloodbath's going to come, Tucuman, I swear it's coming. The Orishás told me that terrible day is coming, the Ajogún are swirling all around us."

Everyone felt the impact of that prophecy. Knowing about the ferocious powers of the Ajogún from the milk of their black nursemaids, some men crossed themselves, terrified. Me more than anyone; I had been convinced of their talents for a long time. Confronted by my insistence, she had told me of her magic-making and the Yoruba rituals, in whose religion she was a priestess.

But Belgrano did not even weigh the possibility of the mulatto's words foretelling of such catastrophe, and he dismissed her. For quite some time, pride had made him its prey *you are afraid I realize because your hands sweat and tremble you are afraid of everything you make out to be brave but your courage leaves you right away when fear pushes you from below the fear of ending up badly fear they'll think ill of you fear of feeling what you can notice just by looking at you fear of being afraid fear the same fear I feel when I realize that the more I hate you the more bound I am to you.*

Faced with the proximity of the battle, a metamorphosis came over the camp. Everyone's gaze was brighter even in the darkness, and each fiber became tense with an atavistic instinct. Our bodily movements became brisk and precise, as if saving energy for combat. Like just another warrior, she demonstrated those symptoms before the fight. And, as if it were possible, I loved her all the more.

Transformed into a wild beast, she corralled her Sir Genrul in such a way that she came into possession of a rifle that she cared for and handled better than any soldier.

And the horror began... Beloved Junta, respected Junta, citizens of Buenos Aires, if you had only seen our illustrious general playing on the battlefield with little soldiers that bled for real. The sons of prominent citizens, who in May had been toastung with champagne and adorning their hats with little olive branches, died there. To them, I do not believe that it mattered much, but hundreds of blacks and mulattoes also died there. A Paraguayan garrotted a soldier beside me. He had sung all day long, but at that moment blood came from his throat, not songs. Blood as red as mine, as red as yours. What sense did my friend Saavedra find in it when he reviewed the disaster! What little courage he used to oppose the plotters! In an act of misguided bravery he sent me to spy on Belgrano, without giving me any means to stand up to him. As if my mere presence would have magically been able to forestall the disaster. He didn't know how to risk his neck, nor did I.

Wherever you looked in the midst of the bloodshed, there

she was, urging her boys on, firing on the Paraguayans, mingling praises to the Virgin with invocations of mercy from her warrior gods. But the prophecy was inexorably fulfilled.

Whole companies of lancers, Black and Browns, paid with their lives for a debt they had never contracted. The extermination of that race began then and to this day has not ceased. The few who remain alive still do not know what to do with a freedom that, from lack of use, has rusted in their souls.

Faced with our advance into their territory, the tame Paraguayans sacrificed their survival. They burned their harvests and abandoned their homes, leaving us starving in ghost towns where only fat, distracted rats strolled around.

After the defeats in Paraguay and at Tacuarí, Belgrano's frustration was unleashed. He stopped hiding it and, as always, I was the target he favored. He knew that, assisted by the darkness of night and with the complicity of a messenger scout, I would make known to the Junta the truth and not the delirious version that he obliged me to write about his defeats, whose explanations he found in the will of God. There is nothing more dangerous than irrationality displayed in His name.

And since the price of mistakes is never paid for by the powerful, the ideologues of that expedition took no responsibility for that useless bloodbath. When Buenos Aires could choose for the first time, it elected the path of force, thus demonstrating a scorn for the hinterlands, which would forever be the bloody divide that runs through our history.

But thanks to my confidential reports to Saavedra, I did manage for Belgrano to be stripped of his beloved titles and honors, and to be brought to trial, so that he would have to account for his numerous blunders.

We had to begin our return in subhuman conditions. With the failure steeped into my bones, I discovered to my surprise that my heart was with that hungry, untidy group of men who had given up singing.

Given that I was one who had always allowed myself to be dominated by reading so as to not see reality, I only knew about revolutions and heroism from books and café talk. There in Paraguay my old refuge was broken into. Now nothing mitigated the lacerating reality of having been in a war, a real war. War. The word still cuts my tongue and shreds my heart. It was in Paraguay where I smelled gunpowder and blood for the first time. Sharp odors that in time become customary. I used the rifle they gave me and I killed to not be killed. The sad eyes of a boy, surprised to see the red flower my bullet put in his chest, still pursue me, asking why. In that way I woke up forever to the real world. And in truth it was much more terrifying and necessary than fiction.

Her person began to seem familiar around town

Everything was determined from the beginning: her birth, her battles, her dead. Everything was traced out from the outset and would continue even after María Kumbá's death.

Linked as she was to her soul through the gaze of her spirits, she knew beforehand where she ought to be at each moment, and she never missed an appointment, not in war, or in peace time, not in storms, or in calm. She always knew how to bring together her time and her place. She was warrior, mother, lover, friend, according to what was demanded of her. But without ever ceasing to be María Kumbá, a mulatto freed from a slavery most people took for granted, a warrior in this new American land that was being born day by day with an uncertain destiny. A poor relation without deserving to be one, she was present at the birth of a nation that was wealthy without knowing it.

María went around before 5:00 PM in a whirlwind of promises, holding close to her the basket full of almond candies that at "maté time" were indispensable in the houses of numerous clients. The sweets included chayote, guava or quince, an exquisite merchandise that after their crinkly, white wrapping had dried, rested on a wicker bed. She learned the secret from old Luis, who died without knowing that with his ancestral recipes he had achieved culinary perfection.

Her incessant walking around the streets led her to discover the secrets of the town and its barrios. Every nook daily became familiar. Children in rags, delicate maidens, pallid intellectuals, wealthy matrons, old coachmen. They were all her customers and a coin wasn't always the means to be one. When they saw her silhouette from a distance prophesying sweetness, they halted their progress to dig ecstatically into her basket, looking for their favorite flavor.

That was how she discovered, to her surprise, large

numbers of women of all ages, blacks and mulattoes in the majority, whom life had left forgotten in a corner. And she immediately made common cause with those less-than-fortunate women who populated the streets of Santa María de los Buenos Aires, sleeping in doorways and eating the leftovers from the market, which they sometimes had to pay for with their pathetic, emaciated bodies. All of them marginal to that incipient government that already carried the seeds of indifference.

Ancient in the bloom of youth, toothless and prostituted, some didn't even have the luck to have been slaves and in that way enjoy a master's sheltering roof. Sooner or later, unless liberating death reached them first, eventually they crowded hospitals, shelters, or jails, repositories of leftover human beings. The helplessness of those women, and the ghostly sunken-eyed children they carried clinging to their skirts and their luck! She would be their daily consolation because anger grew inside her when she saw the pain of those others, who she also was.

Obatalá, the great, who belongs to the world. Obatalá the Orishá of authority who is as favored as pure honey. Obatalá, save me! Alone, I don't know how to save myself.

Well, a while ago I was telling you that my hunches never failed me. I prob'ly have gotten the reputation for being distrustful, but I've never been wrong. Look here, excepting only with Manuel Dorrego, that young scoundrel who was everywhere at the same time. From the beginning I told my Sir Genrul that he was going to bring about some surprising thing. I always saw him looking like omo-aiye, but he used to get angry with me and told me I was long in the tooth.

So you see that I made no mistake. I'm going to tell you about it. Back from Ayohuma, my Sir Genrul could hardly keep himself up on his feet. The sadness about leaving the Army, that was killing him. And what do you think that rascal Dorrego did? As he was in charge of the forces at Santiago del Estero at that time, when we passed through there, he looked for a poor lunatic, dressed him up in Sir Genrul's uniform, and set him loose to stroll around the streets.

How it did pain my Goldilocks! And what do you want me to tell you? Right then and there I disgraced myself, and I set a curse on him that I had never put on anybody. So's you be aware, I always did know how to finish off a human being. There in El Tambor witchcraft was like a sister to me. Don't forget that until I married, I lived there with Mama Basilia. And if I hadn't cursed anybody before, it was because I never wished nobody ill, and the Olorishás prohibited us from bringing harm, but evil exists and we have to know how to stop it before it stops us. That time it roused up from my soul, and I asked Olorúm for him to die a horrible death. And though he might singe me in hell and Shangó might not love me anymore, I don't repent it, even today. Whoever made my Sir Genrul suffer was my enemy. Truth be that that shrimpy

*Dorrego was nice like nobody else and he made me laugh
with his crazy ideas. But he'd hurt my Sir Genrul real deep
and I wasn't going to forgive him. The only one I pardoned
for his hatred was Gregorio Rivas, because it was such a
strange hatred from so long before that it wasn't my business.
Sir Genrul hated him jest as much, and that joined them up
so close that they didn't even realize they couldn't live one
without the other. At times I became jealous from such
neediness, but afterwards I scolded myself. I couldn't be
jealous of them.*

*And now you are going to believe I'm a witch. I got news
that last year they shot tiny Dorrego, and yup, he died like he
lived. Don't go thinking of me as a witch, but it's a fact that
from when I was a young girl Mama Basilia initiated me in
the Yoruba religion, the one we brought from Africa, not the
crossing-yourself one.*

*She didn't ask me if I wanted to or not. She thought for
me, she always said. She knew I had Shangó inside me. She
learned it the very night I was born. So she began to teach
me everything she knew. Real early in the mornings we'd go
close to the river where nobody could see us, and she didn't
let up telling me everything there was about our gods. About
Orunmila, son of the gods, the perfect king who turns death
away; about Eshú, the one who carries human offerings to
the gods; about Yemoja, mother of the fishes and of the waters
on the Earth. But above all about Shangó, my father, the
warrior and protector, him of the great royal drums who
protects against misfortunes. But what she most repeated to
me was the humility a body should have to be a Babalawo.*

*Months went by like that, all those things swirling around
in my head, and I couldn't stop praying to all of them, begging
them to make me a true priestess. After a short time, she gave
me the ilekes that are something like necklaces so it could be
known if you were able to become a Babalawo.*

*When she reckoned that I was ready to receive Shangó,
she took me to a secret place, far from people, and I went*

three days without eating. When I returned I felt closer to the gods than to people. In the hall she and the old witchdoctors, all dressed in white, were waiting for me. It was a night in December and the heat added to the heat from the candles. In a clay tureen there were green bananas and tobacco washed and scrubbed with sarsaparilla water, and rum, all Shangó's yuyo. On one side there was the rooster they'd sacrificed, with the blood dripping into a wooden bowl. The drums commenced to beat and the people with me started to dance, giving thanks to Shangó. Mama Basilia, who was my iyawo, my godmother, presented me to Shangó. I was kneeling and trembling with emotion, the prayers weren't stopping, and we all asked for the offerings to be accepted and for them to set the gods to moving about: aboru, aboye, aboisise, everybody sang and all of me began to tremble. I believe I fainted, as though a lightning bolt had split me in two, and I heard that Shangó was telling me I was his daughter, and I should mind him in everything. And I almost always did...

From then on, I started to see the future and folks' ailments. Jest as soon as I saw a sickly person, right away I knew how to cure him. That never left me, and I cured people all my life.

For all the cuffs Mama Basilia gave me, what I never wanted was to throw the obis for people. I already had enough of seeing what was going to come. I wasn't going to set out to throw obis, those nut shells still being used for divining. Why, it was painful to see the faces of the people who were going to find out about their future. When she died I kept her obis, but not even out of my mind would I divine the future. People hope to hear what they need to. I would throw them for myself, to ask them about my affairs. Result was that I wasn't going to get riled up or scared by the answers, and since they answer right quick, yes or no, I used to ask every now and then. That's how it went for me too.

Right now I'm going to light up a corn cigarillo, after all. Everybody's asleep in the house. Carmen gets mad when

*she sees me smoking and she says I'm too old to be puffing
so much. If she'd have seen me with the pipe and the seegar.
I didn't leave 'em behind even when I went to the river to
wash up. Up there at the North, after the battles, it was a
pleasure to smoke a seegar with the boys. Sir Genrul himself,
who coughed on the smoke, egged us on to light up even
though it was night and the Barbarians could locate us on
account of the embers. Why sometimes we smoked because
we didn't have food, but at least we had something in our
mouths.*

*Shoot, I sure am getting callers tonight! Look, look,
there's my little boy. My Agustín. I had a hunch that so much
humidity was going to get him sick no matter how chubby I
had him. He was going on two years of age and I kept on
having milk for my little calf.*

*'Cause he nursed at all times I had no choice but to take
him with me when I went to the river to wash the clothes that
on Mondays I picked up at the big house. The Missis, to help
me out, gave me her fine things, petticoats and shawls the
girls wore to weekend parties.*

*Winter and summer I passed the time scrubbing, on my
knees in the sand on the bank. At times fighting and throwing
rocks to scare away the little boys lazing around who, out of
sheer peevishness, would throw mud on the clothes jest then
rinsed. But truth is I had fun. We used to get together five or
six neighbor women, each one with her pile of clothes, and
we'd sing all the songs we knew and others we'd invent. Some
were Nagó, others Congolese, who are the gayest. You're not
going to believe me but it's the truth that music gives strength,
even your arms stop aching when you sing. As it comes from
Olorúm, the Orishá of music, he comes down and he makes
the music magic...*

*All the little snotty-noses had a great time too and
splashed along the shore. They got together something like
fifteen infants and the littlest ones, like my Agustín, frolicking
in the water. But that winter, the cold jest got into his tiny*

bones. *He commenced to have a fever with shivers that lasted three days. He stayed quiet in my arms. What didn't the Babalawo do to save him! But he couldn't. It seemed my little negrito jest wanted to go away with his grandparents and with Obatalá, the greatest of the great. That night the batá drums didn't stop beating and calling for the Orishás so's they could prepare the way for him... Yemoja, Oyá, Oshún, not a one was missing. They had to use force, all of them, to make me open my arms and let go of my little son.*

Manuel and I, we stayed with our eyes dry from so much weeping. I swear to you that from then on, I'm missing a part of my heart. A day doesn't go by that I don't remember him, so tender, pure laughter, my Agustín.

I close my eyes and feel his tiny arms on my neck... The scent of a suckling calf I liked so much even comes to me. To make him sleep, I would cradle him without getting tired, jest from the pure pleasure of smelling him and to smell him till we both stayed sleeping like we was one.

SIX

The moment to face my own faults had come

We returned to Buenos Aires in the midst of widespread indifference. Defeat is an obscene spectacle and makes heads turn away. A year had passed since the Revolution, and the city was no longer the same. Most of the leaders were dead, in exile, or being persecuted. The first Junta had disappeared, and now the Grand Junta governed, having humiliated the provincials the year before.

My friend, Cornelio Saavedra, continued as president, vindicated in April by a populace that went out into the streets singing his name. Creoles, country folk, peasants, and militiamen anointed him the undisputed leader, to the disgust of Moreno's followers, who could not stomach the effusions of the commoners, nor their smell.

Our people had finally completed that work, as tardy as it was necessary. The inestimable Dr. Mariano Moreno died under mysterious circumstances on the high seas, circumstances so mysterious that the news was barely even murmured in that port city where, at one time, the measure of his intelligence was overwhelming.

But the air was dense with intrigue. Something new began to divide Buenos Aires. It was not Moreno's followers against Saavedra's, but something much worse. The waters had separated between Porteños and provincials. They did not band together to curse the Spaniards, but instead began to fight each other for power like dogs after a bone. So we resuscitated Cain and Abel, and it was then that God damned us forever.

Young revolutionaries went out into the streets in rowdy groups that sang anti-government songs, angering merchants and street vendors who were used to the serenity of the status quo. They met in the Café de Marco, raising their voices against the cowardly president of the Grand Junta who was trying to make a bloodless revolution. And living under the same sky became impossible.

Then destiny turned the tables and luck set itself against us. The clamorous defeat of our troops in Huaqui made it indispensable to send someone to bring order to that disjointed army and to us, that is, the barbarians of the North. And on the basis of a tangled, fraudulent voting that went on all night long, the Grand Junta decided by a majority that their president was the one for that mission.

The maneuver to remove Saavedra from office was so obvious and clumsy that none of us could understand how our leader submitted himself to it so sheepishly. He could have remained, but chose exile. He lacked the grit or had ideals to spare. My poor friend Saavedra; after his Palm Sunday came his crucifixion. Those who gave him an ovation in April, in September apathetically let him depart on his way to oblivion. How true it is that revolutions devour their sons without delay!

After his departure, it was easy to silence us, already broken, and a short time later with no warning, a triumvirate, lackey to the Patriotic Clan, took over.

Meanwhile, Belgrano's trial was in full swing. It was one of the hardest blows the Goldilocks suffered in his life. Proclamations were issued calling for those who might have some accusation to make against him.

Immediately after our arrival in Buenos Aires, María disappeared from my side and ran off to find her daughters. One morning, crazed with fury, she nearly knocked down the door of my boarding house with her pounding.

"I swear by San Benito that I can't believe it, Tucuman. Those people are insane. Who's gonna speak up opposing my Sir Genrul? Don't leave him alone. He's going to die of grief."

It was grotesque to see that warrior I had fallen in love

with wringing her apron, her eyes full of tears. I squeezed her in my arms with all my strength, rocking her like a little girl. Her closeness once again awoke my feelings. God, how I needed her!

For fear she would stick a knife in me if she discovered that I was the ringleader of the plan to destroy him, I swore that I would dedicate my life to help her Sir Genrul.

And despite our threatening witnesses and buying them off, no one testified against Belgrano. One by one the officers and soldiers of his expedition appeared before the government singing the praises of their leader.

María served as the point of contact, and there was not a single member of the Battalion of the Black and Browns who did not come forward to make a statement. They came before the tribunal with tears in their eyes and swore by their gods that "Sir Genrul" was the bravest of leaders. Even in the face of my pain as I saw my revenge disappear, I knew the government had no recourse but to absolve him and return his beloved titles and honors to him.

As is known, bad news does not come alone but in droves; days later a letter for me came from Tucumán. No sooner did I see it on the nightstand than I knew there was pain inside it, and I was not wrong. In a letter with ink streaked in places, Bernardo announced our father's death. They had found him lifeless in the same bed where, years before, his loving Indian wife had died in childbirth, the newborn in her arms.

This time there was no bloodshed, shouts, tears, or other excesses. Francisco Rivas imposed his severe dominion over our emotions even in death. Having foreseen his end the year before did not lessen the orphanhood that enveloped me. I no longer had even him to be responsible for my failures. The moment to face my own faults had arrived, and I envied Bernardo who had closed all his accounts with our father before he closed his eyelids.

My brother took responsibility for the obese widow and

her two daughters, who accepted the condolences of all our neighbors in Tucumán, dressed in black from head to foot in a crepe-filled house, with furniture and mirrors covered in black drapes.

The lights were lowered and, surrounded by burning tapers, his viewing went on for an entire day. First, the prayers of nine nights, and then mourning for thirty days, all were a social event that everyone took advantage of in a city that, without knowing it, was experiencing its last peaceful times.

For Bernardo now began the difficult task of administering the numerous assets of our family, without assistance, since Ignacio was in the Vatican, and I, as always, was in any place but the right one. He cursed the luck that postponed his wedding to Dolores, his young fiancée, until a nebulous date in the future.

I saw Belgrano again a few months after his return from Paraguay. His glance and mine became knotted together. The blood spilled in those horrible battles was yet another means to fasten us. We were like heads and tails on the coin called reproach.

Anxiety had left visible marks on his face, and his health had deteriorated noticeably. The death of his bosom buddy Moreno had sunk him into a ponderous silence, full of accusations, and the once impeccable blue broadcloth jacket was now seen to be loose-fitting and slovenly, showing, with the former, the loss of weight he'd suffered, and in the latter, the absence of María.

In an attempt to repair the damage from his trial, and lacking another individual who would be so popular with his men, the Triumvirate named him to lead a new military mission: to patrol the banks of the Paraná, the Spaniards' new objective.

I moved heaven and earth to go along. I wielded all manner of absurd arguments: my father's death, my need to be in the North in order to see my brother, my proven experience as an administrator of arms and munitions. The others, the real arguments, I kept to myself. But they so empowered my words that to get me out of the way they placed me in charge of armaments, munitions, and artillery, without consulting Belgrano, in spite of knowing that I was a friend of Saavedra's. I was supposed to inventory existing supplies and take charge of their replacements, as I had done before *it's not goin' to be easy to get rid of me you've never done it your debt gets bigger you owe me the betrayal of my friend Saavedra he didn't deserve what he got the hatred I feel for you keeps me alive you hate me too because you know I'm a witness and that I'll tell my people all you're going to do you make out to be tough but you can't with me when you dictate your reports I correct them I change the words in them I dwell on the long paragraphs I try to perfect my writing I make sure my marks are unmistakable, unique that they stand out among the hundreds of reports that will certainly end up in some shit file chewed on some day by rats I hate your signature I hate those exaggerated curlicues in your signature I hate that pen you lean on to feel important but I swear to you that with my writing the truth I'll find a way to be part of history too.*

Since it could not be any other way, María came with us. It seemed natural, and even necessary, to see her arrive greeting everybody like a queen, proud and happy, carting her bag heavy with soaps, amulets, and her flat iron. Several of us stood with our mouths hanging open when we saw two replicas of her appear behind her. They were Teresa and Antonia, the young daughters she spoke to me so much about those nights after we made love together, when the heat and memories would not allow us to sleep, and dawn surprised us with our maté and our souls in our hands.

For nothing in the world did I want to miss Belgrano's reaction to seeing the arrival of that trio of intruders who in their very clothing seemed to stir up all existing colors and others not yet invented. But I was not able to give myself the pleasure of seeing him blush. He was no longer as he had been. He fell into lengthy silences that not even the disorder that reigned among the troops could break him out of. With his gaze off into the distance, in his reserve he did not even seem to recognize their presence, and that was the precise measure of his sloppiness.

We again departed from an increasingly violent Buenos Aires, with three mulattoes instead of one. We did not know it yet, but their hands would be the ones to save the lives of many of us way off in Vilacapugio and Ayohuma.

My happiness was so great that I forgot about my father's death, Saavedra's exile, my hatred for Belgrano and, like just another Negro, I departed for Santa Fe, with a few drum sticks and mazacayas hidden in my belongings.

Nothing would happen by chance in the life of María Kumbá

Nor was it a coincidence that her two men had the same name. Her two Manuels who needed her so much, the light and the dark. She who also was the one to close their eyelids at the end.

With how many dreams did she begin her new life beside her husband, her black Manuel! The two of them together put up a dwelling that was their safe haven. The two of them together made a living going out into the streets of the town. And with him she had the three children who were her pride.

Manuel wanted Father Antonio to marry them, brought up as he was under the serene protection of the parish of Montserrat and himself a pious member of the brotherhood of San Benito. A devout follower of the saint closest to Olorúm, María accepted, pleased to show off her best dress as she stood before the altar that Manuel had been responsible for keeping clean and neat for many years.

After they left the church joined in wedlock, they went to Mama Basilia's, who was almost blind and clearly ready to shortly go join the gods who had always been her companions. She brought their two heads together, made the gesture of a cord binding their two bodies together, and from the same bowl fed them the seeds that from time immemorial symbolized a definitive union.

María had no choice but to survive all of her loved ones. How many of them died in her arms! Were the Orishás testing her perhaps? Because if that's the way it was, she passed their tests with flying colors. And for all of them she had been the answer to their perplexity at the last moment. Each one of them carried away the image of her dark, tearful eyes, full of pain and understanding that helped them die.

Her mother, her little son, Mama Basilia, her two

Manuels, and so many of her boys, whose faces became jumbled together and blurred in ungodly visions...

They all needed her at their life's end. She kneeled next to them with her aroma of herbs and protection, and closed their eyelids with the tips of her fingers, a gesture that combined alchemy, ancient rituals, and dolorous love. In her arms their dying bodies received a last breeze of energy that calmed their fear of the passage.

Dark Manuel was her companion and the father of her children. He knew, always did, that he should let her spread her wings to fly to her appointments. And he loved her placidly until his death. Raised by Franciscan priests, he existed in an undefined condition, between slave and freeman, that because of his kindness was never tiresome. That was no obstacle for him to learn a trade made to fit his timidity. He was the best cobbler in the barrio of El Tambor, which allowed him to maintain his family with dignity and, with an innocent ostentation, he belonged to the brotherhood of San Benito, all together a sign of prosperity. That was the only show of vanity he permitted himself during his life and it allowed him to have a dignified funeral and a few masses said for the salvation of his soul, something that would never have offended God.

For him, joining his life with María's was an undeserved gift of the Orishás, and he loved her with a love so great and powerful that only at his side, with sad remorse for not reciprocating his love, could she rest from the weariness she'd already suffered and from the fatigue yet to come.

With such joy she gave birth to her three children! She threw them into life with the same joy as during their conception, and thus she erased the memory of her own haphazard birth on the kitchen stoop of the big house.

There were three appointments that consecrated her as a propagator of offspring. There were three encounters of life and blood in which she gave everything, up to her last breath. Lying on the corn-husk tick that she prepared with the care of a nesting bird for the big moment, she could barely contain the scream that fought to escape from her throat. Bathed in sweat, her fists clenched, she whispered invocations to Obatalá to help her give birth to her child. And all the Orishás surrounded her like a protective blanket, giving her the strength to release that bit of flesh from her insides that was so much hers and yet so foreign.

What a woman she felt she was when they placed her firstborn on her stomach, skin of chocolate, still tied by the cord that came up through her legs! And for a magic instant it was another link with all those women who since the beginning of time have offered their lives to give birth.

That was the way she joyfully went through maternity, nurturing her children with kisses and love. And anyone passing her shack at dusk might slow his step to hear the lullabies in Nagó she sang to put her children to sleep. The cadence was so tender and doleful, the voices of her grandmother and her mother together with hers were heard so clearly, that the melancholy coming from the melody fused with the magic twilight of El Tambor in the heart of that casual listener.

**Shangó has come. Shangó, do not argue with me,
I am not one of those who are against you.
Let all human beings come and meditate.
My Lord, owner of the big, royal drums,
protect us from misfortune, protect us
from illness.**

*As I was telling you, I can't say that Governor Viamonte
didn't feel like helping me. Well-intentioned he always was,
that man. But imagine, him being so important, how's he
going to have time to remember about all of the paperwork
concernin' a sick old mulatto. I tell you that he even wanted
to have them give me a Lady Captain's pension and said he's
going to have them send me a learned little gentlemen so I
could tell him my life and him write it out. By golly, I say,
such a clamor they want to make jest now when I'm about to
die. How come they didn't remember when I really had no
money not even to get food with! That's how I was for a time
when I returned from the North.*

*By then I could jest barely walk from the pain I had in my
leg. Imagine, the wound they gave me in Ayohuma was still
red. Did I already tell you about that butchery? That was a
time the bedlam put the fright in a person. I swear, wherever
a body turned there was blood, the hollering was terrible.
The cannon smoke got into your eyes and left jest about
anybody blind. I don't know at what moment that clumsy
horseman appeared, saber in hand. I could jest barely jump
backwards, spiriting my body away. But the son of his mother
was quicker and I felt real clear when the blade cut into my
leg. I fell down from it and then I don't remember any more.
The Virgin helped me and I fainted.*

*Well, the doctor told me later that the blade went in
almost to the bone. I'm telling you that I was with that leg all
gimpy till now, but in that time when I jest returned from the
North was when it acted up the most. That's why I started*

holding my hand out around the cathedral, around the Plaza Victoria, or close to Town Hall. I can't tell you the shame it brought on me at first! I would put a black shawl over my head so's nobody'd recognize me, and I didn't even pray to the Orishás for fear they'd come down and scold me. The tricks life plays! Auntie María made into a lame beggar with no roof over her, 'cause from leaving it abandoned so much my shack already had another family living there with so many little ones that I didn't have the guts to kick them out.

You might say people's good and they hadn't forgot about my almond cakes. They all helped me out and Teresa and me we got through that bad time. A little bit of herbs here, a bit of corn there, nobody abandoned this despairing mulatto.

When I returned to El Tambor, Nagó people helped me to start up again with the almond cakes. In a bit I commenced to gather together a few coins and I put up this shack the way I like it, close to the river. If it weren't that you might take me for a crazy woman, I'd swear the water talks to me at times. It tells me things about places and people I don't know and it leaves me dreaming dreams so strange and pretty they make me feel like another person altogether.

But I wasn't the same as I was before. My skeleton had got delicate on me and my grief didn't leave me no peace. Every morning I had to do a cure with scrubbings of henbane and a tea of hound's tongue with a tincture of short buchu to be able to go out with the basket of almond cakes that weighed more and more, as though it was cannon balls I was carrying. By some miracle I tolerated it till I sold the last one so's I could come back to lay myself down in this hammock.

I lived that way whilst I could, a few short years, that's all. It was harder and harder for me to walk, and I was already so weak that I couldn't even mix the sweets for the almond cakes... And my, jest when things was going that way, Teresa out of the blue gets married and I'm left with no help to make the dough. No, don't think the poor little thing was a bad daughter. She and her husband went off to live in

Montserrat and they had a shoal of children. I couldn't go about sticking my nose in, 'cause poor people always jest get by. What's worse, I was mighty sad, missing my Sir Genrul so much. They'd sent him off to Europe. They say he'd gone happy; hadn't even bid me farewell. It was like he didn't need me anymore. But that was what he believed; he couldn't even imagine how much he'd need me later.

A day didn't go by that I didn't think about him and I would commence to leaking tears. I was feeling like I didn't have no life in the mornings when I'd wake up and realize I wasn't going to see him. I had no wish to get up, I swear to you.

And believe me, one blessed day I couldn't make any more almond cakes. Not even begging for help from San Benito or the Orishás was I able to gather my strength to roll out the dough. I wept until nighttime. I couldn't believe that after I'd done so many things in my life that I would be so useless. Awful fierce it is when the body grows surly and doesn't want to obey. I fell asleep tired of swearing, and Mama Basilia appeared to me. She was mad at me and asked me how I'd forgotten the powers I had and those I had used before to help so many people. Why had Shangó put me in this world if it wasn't to help those who needed me? Ought to make me ashamed to go sniffling about in that way; it didn't seem like Kumbá. And she went on scolding me in dreams. She said that it wasn't shameful if I needed to beg to get by, and if I continued making a fool of myself, the Orishás was going to get me for forsakening them.

I woke up so scolded that from that night on, real quiet, I went back to tending to people in the barrio like Mama Basilia'd done. I couldn't be such a fool any more and I commenced to heal folks. If their problem was nerves, I had them make a tea of tobacco, marjoram, and path-openers, which are Elegba's erinle, the Orishá who cures the palsy. If it was a woman who was suffering because she couldn't get pregnant, I had her dress in blue and sent her to the bank of a river to make an offering to Yemoja of black and white sugar that she should cast and say at the same time: "YEMOJA ASE'SUN, ASE'SUN YEMOJA," at least ten times. That means: "Yemoja is the busting out of spring, the busting out of spring is Yemoja." It never failed. They all returned weeping to thank me for the child that was moving inside them. That was the work I liked to do best. If the patient was an old man who had his lungs eaten up by so much smoking, I sent him to the cemetery on a moonless night to pour red wine and rum on the dirt for Oyá, and for ten days to prepare a tea with star apple and yucca. If he didn't come back to see me, it was on account of how some are cowards who wet their pants from jest thinking about going to the holy ground. All in all, if it also saved his children the funeral...

But don't fool yourself, as a young girl I was tougher than many men. When I went to Paraguay with my Sir Genrul, jest imagine what I had to go through to get used to such a life. Truth be told, not even today do I know where I found the courage to face him and ask him to take me along. My heart was jumping in my chest when I saw him so close to me, jest like in my dreams, but then, if I reached out my hand, I could touch him. How pretty my Sir Genrul was. What I didn't do for him. You're going to laugh, but so's to give him pleasure I stayed like a statue seeming interested during masses he had us listen to, long, all of them. I saw him happy so seldom; sadness flowed out of his eyes every now and then without him even knowing it. I wonder what he was thinking about? I believe it was about that great pain that pierced into his heart that he told me about while we waited for the enemy there in Ayohuma, on those nights so dark you couldn't even see your hands. I was astonished by what I heard. It was so terrible that I don't know how I didn't suspect, being so full of takings. It only came to me to pat him slowly on the shoulder like I was trying to tell him I understood. 'Course I know that the heart takes no orders. Don't lick your chops. Not even out of my mind will I tell you about it. Because that night I also swore to him that I'd carry his secret to the grave, and take it for granted that I'm going to do it.

Do you think he might have loved me as much as I loved him? I believe so, what do you want me to say? He wasn't much for showing how he felt. Seems like that's how they raised him, with so many brothers and spending all that time with priests. They sure don't laugh at nothing, not even if you tickle them. The longer their face, the more saints they believe in. What I am certain about is that the poor soul needed me like nobody's business during that time. I was his friend, his nurse, his comrade, and a whole bunch of other things that only he and me knew about. Though I might wish to, I don't know how to explain to you what was happening to me and my little Goldilocks. It seemed like he had what I was missing and the other way around too. I gave him what he needed. But he didn't want to realize that he needed me, even if it was to chide me when he was angry about something or other. Another one he needed was Tucuman. He got sicker when, after coming back from the North, Tucuman stayed home with his brother, who seemed scared, as though he was seeing spirits all the time.

'Course we fought too, don't be silly. Sometimes he made out to be angry and protested, saying to me that I was a busybody who didn't leave him in peace, but when I became offended and left furious, right then and there he'd have me sent for. Jest seeing him my anger passed and I laughed all by myself.

Oh, my Sir Genrul, how clear you come into my sight.

SEVEN

The nation was being born

We again departed from Buenos Aires, this time toward Santa Fe. The government had commissioned us to manufacture high-caliber artillery for the defense of the Paraná.

With past anxieties only partially scarred over, our spirits became light again and smiling Negroes and mulattoes formed columns behind the Sir Genrul they adored with the same intensity with which he detested them.

We came to the shore of the Paraná on a day whose heat was so asphyxiating that our libertarian ideas had evaporated. In Rosario, the artillery dragoons, soaking with sweat and lethargy, and without the slightest interest, half-heartedly finished the task of fortifying the river to block the passage of the Spanish flotilla, already dangerously close.

Just then, looking at the Paraná, Manuel Belgrano awoke from his torpor, and before the sun set on the first day after our arrival, he had already driven us crazy with orders and counter-orders. He was in his medium, surrounded by so many blindly obedient men.

When he discovered me among his people he did not hide his vexation: "Well, Rivas...what perseverance you have! Do not tell me that you have exchanged your pen for a rifle. What are you going to invent this time?"

"Nothing, Your Grace. Obeying your orders gives me more satisfaction than my writings." Only when I made a simulated bow did he recognize the deception.

I was not going to put up with nights like the past ones in Paraguay, and I put my leather-thonged cot in the officer's tent. I dedicated myself to pursuing María, and she went after him, and he after everyone. The pieces on the board of play returned to their places.

79

María and I reinitiated our nocturnal ceremonies. Sometimes I was the one who arrived first at the beach farthest from the camp, and I stayed sitting there in the sand, trembling with expectation until she would silently approach from behind. First it was her arm around my neck, then her unmistakable scent. We submerged ourselves in unsuspected abysses, daring to explore deeper and deeper in prohibited territories. Tense, vibrant, young, expert, wise, virgin. Reality and imagination were indistinguishable. I said goodbye to her until the next moon, grateful to her for receiving me in her abyss, for allowing me to feel the pulsing of my blood.

A somewhat loony Spaniard named Monasterio directed the making of the armaments. It was said of him that after he slit the throat of an unfaithful wife, he escaped from Toledo and hid in the storeroom of a ship loaded with merchandise from Castile. He would take charge of everything, starting from scratch. Something like a magic trick. And the damned fellow did it.

Belgrano divided us into patrols and, excited at the prospect of the surprising mission charged to us, we would go out every morning to beg from the solicitous neighbors any kind of junk to melt down, which we then transported in carts and on mules. Old bedsteads, small basins, spurs, hardware, keys, candelabra, those were the contributions that with our laughter and off-color jokes we dragged to the camp.

Soon the place turned into the forge of Vulcan, and during 15 days with their 15 nights the fire was kept alive by the demise of the trees from that place.

Without consulting anyone, María stepped forward to be Monasterio's helper, on the condition that she could be rid of the washing and ironing. Different from the majority of us, who could not tolerate being close to that inferno, she moved around next to those cauldrons all day long. It was impressive to see her carrying that glowing metal without burning herself.

"You're going to burn to a crisp, María. You're getting

crazier and crazier," I forecast to her, worried about her much-loved flesh.

When she saw my fear she took pity, and laughing with those teeth that made their way around my body at night she confessed one of her secrets: before going to work she rubbed her hands three times in a row with a mixture of red arsenic, alum, the juice of white stonecrop, and the resin released by the bay tree. By doing that, it was impossible to feel the effects of the fire.

And thus began my custom of asking her about the secrets of her magic and her spells and she of revealing them to me. It was what served me well for my final vengeance, without her then suspecting it.

We dedicated ourselves, body and soul, to melting and fusing the metal that, like a liquid fire, distributed itself in the molds from whence came bullets, cannons, and shiny mortars.

After an incredible period of 15 days, I proudly expedited a report to Buenos Aires that notified the Triumvirate that we awaited the enemy fully equipped. With no aid from them, we were able to rely on so many pieces of artillery we could not stop polishing with the cuffs of our uniforms so that we felt rich, invincible, winners. Yes, though it is hard for me to believe, I wore mine without complaint at that time, and I was just another soldier who polished those round shapes I saw come into being.

But after having finished the armaments, we went back to having no objectives, and our siestas in Santa Fe began to seem to us as ponderous as guilt. Faced with so much general boredom, I initiated a campaign to denigrate that ill-humored general who had no goals and who submersed us in uncertainties in a humid, slumbering land.

As I promised at the beginning of this tale, if I want to be honest with you, I ought to recognize that in Rosario de Santa Fe, Belgrano was naturally intuitive. He had perceived that in the heat and absence of food, spirits were drooping and no one believed in the revolutionary cause. The feeling of power looking at so many armaments was as ephemeral as our full stomachs. Then he conceived of a ceremony that was theatrical, but effective. As if by the art of magic, at the moment of inaugurating the batteries that we had made with such rapidity, he had them display a flag with the colors of our cockade, sewn by candlelight by the mulatto women the night before.

Lining those embankments under the twilight sky, mouths agape like those of the curious neighbors who approached, we saw our flag with two colors hoisted, a flag mixed with the sky. And never again the Spanish flag. I forgot about hatred, rancor, and passions that, like scabs, covered over my understanding. The images became blurred with tears, and a feeling grew in me that was so powerful that it displaced all other known feelings. The nation was being born and, blinded by personal passions, I could not see it. My father and his disdain were appropriate. I would never manage to stay abreast of events. I asked myself *what the hell am I doing crying over any old thing I'm fed up with crying fed up with feeling sorry about the death of my father who never loved me fed up with crying over the flag that sends chills up my spine I was more comfortable with my hatred you get accustomed to old clothes you don't have to take care of because they're old that know too much because they're old now I'm crying over any old thing like a little queer please God like a queer not me no when I simply hated you it was easier now everything is complicated I don't know having so many feelings all at once I don't have time it's difficult I don't want to hatred expels you and is quick-witted*

When I should have shouted "Viva la Patria," I could not. A tight knot like animosity closed my throat, and my heart had to come to my aid. My voice was so intense that it blew to pieces the pent-up hurt and sentiments that kept me from being committed to whatever caused me pain.

I did not know what my place was, or my task, or vocation. But I was sure of my love for that newborn flag. I promised to never neglect it, and since then I have kept my pledge.

That night, spirits were raised so high that despite the scarcity of stores, no one made a move to withdraw to their bed. You could hear the strumming of a guitar in the distance, playing counterpoint to another one even farther away. Around the campfires, the troops celebrated the new flag. A voice rose in the air and the stanzas of a gaucho ballad silenced every sound. The hearty applause mixed with the frenetic beat of a bombo drum that called out for a dancer skilled in Malambo. Two experts jumped up and with the contortions of their feet they accomplished impossible moves. On the other side of the camp, a response like a challenge began in the music and dance of blacks and mulattoes. Sticks, mazacayas, and chico drums started to resound in the night, the euphoria aided by corn mash and grain alcohol—which never were lacking, despite inspections—spread all around. And a "tapada" started up with tambor drums and bass drums in which they both argued and made friends with all their brother drums. That night a mix of races found the insignia they would gratefully die for.

All of a sudden I felt a hand on my shoulder shaking me and a voice prodded by fear: "Tucuman, quick! Sir Genrul is real sick." María's tone left no room for doubts. Stretched out on his cot, immobile in the wan light of a lantern, his profile was so sharp that he seemed to be a cadaver.

He breathed with difficulty, his face slick with sweat, his damp hair plastered to his temples. The bloody vomiting that he attempted to hide was more and more frequent. No matter how much he was tormented with infusions of pelojilla and box-leaved barberry, the spasms' red fury did not let up.

There emanated from him a helplessness so moving that I could understand the mulatto's singlemindedness about caring for his most minute desires. A scant feeling of pity tried to make its way through the tangle of emotions that awoke in me. I denied it. The depth of my anger was too great. Who would think to challenge—equally suicidal or insane—the cynical Triumvirate by inventing a flag? For sure the fear had made him sick *you vomit blood I'm happy let's see if you die now once and for all but there's no way at night I hear you turning in your cot then my frightened little mulatto girl you come loaded up with magic and yuyos to cure your Manuelito you sing plead sweat you deliver yourself to your rituals and I don't exist any more for you what are you waiting for in order to die I say that way I'd be your sole master pretty negrita I want to be your slave your dog your horse but tied up licking you smelling you all my life.*

I rattled my brains. I was not going to resign myself to sharing my mulatto who never did understand that he was not going to look at her as a woman.

"He's been sick for several days. It's the damned fever that won't leave him in peace. If he goes on like this, he's going to die on me. Ifá doesn't hear me."

Between the two of us we managed to undress him, peeling off his drenched clothes, without his regaining consciousness. I left María freshening his face, while she, still angry at the inactivity of the gods, murmured unintelligible Yoruba chants. From her eres, shells that I later learned were only used in desperate cases on account of the great power they wield, she pulled out fern seeds gathered at the beginning of the midnight bells during the festivities of San Juan. Poor María! Her Sir Genrul used up her store of magic seeds.

I left the tent and went to sit far from the hubbub that reigned over the camp. As only it can, reality had given me a blow. We were under the command of a dying man who was not even fighting for his life.

The news that we had a new mission and that Belgrano would take charge of the Army of Upper Peru could not have come at a better moment. The official version was that he should replace General Pueyrredón, who had fallen from his horse and was dying from the blow his lungs suffered. But later we were informed of the truth.

The first day of March that year, we set out for the north with a pallid, dissipated Belgrano laid out inside a carriage, so weak that he was in no condition to lead even a children's serenade.

I had to bear his lack of appetite and María's bad moods during the heat of each day's march toward Yatatso, where Pueyrredón was waiting for us, apparently as sick as Belgrano. They had me fed up with their squabbles like long-married couples who cannot tolerate each other. She fell into disapproving, surly silences, faced with the lack of interest he showed in recovery. She threatened to gather her things and go back to Buenos Aires with her daughters in the first wagon going south, although we all knew that only in death would she abandon us, since her life was in the Army and, more precisely, at the side of her "Sir Genrul."

But no one counted on the force that emanated from Manuel Belgrano, who knew from where? I believe he was happy mortifying his flesh. As if the pain, just like the Jordan, purified him from who knows what sins, present, past, or future.

My heart beat irregularly as we continued north and approached Tucumán.

That humid June the English landed

The yelling announced to El Tambor that the English had landed in La Reducción. Crossing herself, María Kumbá went out into the street knowing that the hour of her destiny had arrived. Her reign began on a gray day that, not by pure coincidence, was in the month both María and Manuel had been born.

She got to Town Hall with her heart beating away in her chest. To defend the city, she too asked for a rifle in the middle of a human anthill where confusion and the shouts of those who had gone to find weapons reigned.

She had never liked the shifty eyes of Viceroy Sobremonte. She had encountered him one day when they asked her to go into the kitchen to deposit the basket of her sweet alfajores there. As she went down one of the corridors she saw him hurriedly leave a bedroom. It was an instant, but sufficient for her to feel a deep displeasure when he settled his viper gaze on her figure. Now she confirmed the repugnance of that time, and she continued to be disgusted by her premonition about his flight, wrapped in the pestilent smell of betrayal.

Poor María Kumbá! Days before, she had experienced the biggest humiliation of her life. Hidden near the plaza market, she cried tears of shame watching that group of bleached-eyed soldiers march to the sound of the reedy music of their bagpipes and, with the complicity of the Spanish authorities, take command of the city's enormous dignity and meager riches.

In all the barrios of the city those tears were shed: No one could put up with such an insult. She never knew that in that brutal invasion some detected a whiff of European sophistication that stood up to so much local barbarism. Fortunately, the applause of their gloved hands was barely audible.

Considering that threat, the inhabitants of Santa María de los Buenos Aires put aside the antagonism between Creoles and Spaniards and united in search of their lost dignity.

In El Tambor the people's will jelled around María, and a commanding power began to emanate from her gaze. Hidden weapons appeared in surprising places, thus fooling the invaders' surveillance. Peddlers, shielded by their apparent timidity, traveled through the barrios carrying weapons in their baskets, handbags, and shoulder bags that the people would later put to use. The wagons that came in from the provinces transporting hides, ponchos, and candies likewise became the perfect hiding places for arms and ammunition. Freedmen and slaves formed militias. All of them gathered in her house to organize the forces in the barrio, and with their hands high in the air, they invoked Olorúm in macumbas so he would guide them in their struggle against the invader. This time the gods must have heard them. They had already once been through the suffering of being robbed of their land; they were not going to be subject to the stronger ones a second time.

In one of the ceremonies, María became the color of the moon and received the instructions from Shangó for her irrefutable mission. She would be the cord that tied together dreams and reality, assisting in the birth of that nation the English now endangered. That night Shangó also announced to her that the moment was near when, for the first time, she would see the face of the man she never stopped dreaming about.

And so, day after day, rumor after rumor, on every street corner, in every barrio, the people went about organizing themselves to retake the city from the hands of pirates more interested in its coffers than in expanding the dominion of their King.

Alliances and conspiracies multiplied. And from El Tambor deadly shadows, good with a knife for being butchers, began to come out aided by nighttime in search of enemy throats to slice clean through.

In the middle of the daily conjuring, the black woman could be seen, immersed in her work, going around the streets of town hawking her alfajores with practiced gestures. But one only needed to approach a little to see in her eyes a ferocity ready to pounce. Her eyes didn't miss even the smallest movement of the enemy troops. And her mouth and ears gave and received messages that were invisible to the invaders but were weaving a deadly net around them.

And the big moment arrived that would mark the birth of a people constituted by that group of men and women. And María Kumbá, a freed mulatto, will be among them, fighting in the streets.

Liniers' ships that have come from Colonia spew forth columns of men. Shouting and howling they advance triumphantly until they get to the Plaza de Toros. From there to the Plaza de la Victoria is but a breath away, the one the English will take, mortally wounded by their rapacious dreams. Men, women, children will conquer the enemy in a ferocious battle that gives birth on the streets to the most beautiful newborn: the Argentine people.

And it will be women like María, or like Manuela from Tucumán, whose ferocity will surprise the men who saw them fight. And baffled respect will awaken in their companions; in the adversary, a surprised incredulity upon discovering that a feminine hand placed the mortal wound, from out of which blood mixed with life escapes, as from a pump.

"Ebo finalizes, Eru gives." Once the offering is accepted, the malignant forces withdraw. (A Yoruba religious saying)

Seems like the heat's got you bad too, don't it? For a time now it's got me up and about. Don't you get tired of listening to me? Who cares about old folks? Seems like nobody's got the time for us, and look here if we don't have things to say.

C'mon, c'mon, so I can tell you about the matter of Tucuman. Hurry up because right now I'm being visited by my deceased. I'm liable not to finish the story for you.

It happens that the night before the battle, I was upset some on account of my Sir Genrul was paler than normal and, jest for a change, he wouldn't even drink a bitter maté if I didn't make him do it. After fighting with him so's he'd eat a bit of stewed corn, I went to converse with Oshoosi and Shangó, the war Orishás. That time they came jest as soon as I had commenced to sing. You could see they was in a rush and feeling like being out, because I had hardly asked them to help us win the battle, when the obi-abata that I'd left near the fire danced an ombligada, belly to belly. I didn't even need to ask. Jest in case you don't know, the obi-abata are the black nut shells for divining that I'd inherited from Mama Basilia, that I never have been separated from. So right then and there I went to bed calm.

The next day it was so hot it stole your breath away. You could hardly even squint your eyes at anything because the glare and the dust we were raising up with so many preparations being made our eyes teared like we was chopping onions for empanadas. And we was going around there while the cannons was firing, all the officers barking different orders. The brawl was so fierce that a group of harebrained Tucumanos didn't recognize the poor Catamarquinos and, thinking they was Barbarians, took off to chase them for a good stretch. But it's not so's you can laugh! The poor gauchos had never seen so much artillery

89

all at once in their lives. They became so scared of the noise that they spooked easy. During these goings on I'm telling you about, and wondering where the Barbarians was, a big wind blew in that lifted up so much dirt we couldn't even see each other's faces. And with that dust it began to be cloudy. I didn't have enough hands to cross myself. It turned dark, like the dead of night. And right there I started to pray to the Orishás, making them remember they'd promised me they was going to make us win the battle.

And here's the best part; peel your ears. First you could feel the noise. It was like a buzzing that came from everywhere. Clouds of them appeared, flying about. Locusts, my friend, thousands of locusts made the afternoon into nighttime. I don't know if they have those bugs in the land of the Barbarians but, by the Virgin del Rosario, those poor devils took such a fright they even dropped their weapons to shoo them off with their hands. But the bugs were nothing if not obstinate, and they fell on them like arrows in their faces and they got into their eyes and mouths, making them go around howling. What a chaos that was! That mass of bugs fell from the sky and covered everything like a carpet.

You can imagine how we capitalized on the advantage the gods had sent us! Even the locusts fought for us! We fell on them, jest like the insects did, and we won the battle, jest as Olorúm had promised. You're not going to tell me that he stinted on his help, because that time it didn't take much for him to come in person to make cowards of those Barbarians.

Truth is I can't complain about that time. I worked like a mule from sunup to sundown, but it gave me pleasure to do it. By then I'd already perked up and I'd brought the two grown children I had left to help me.

It suited me, because it was dangerous to leave them alone so long. At any old moment they was going to show up pregnant with another mouth to feed, but how? And I felt excited, even though I knew that my Sir Genrul was not going to put on a smile for bringing in more blacks. But nothing;

he didn't make any kind of face at all. He seemed to be under a spell, like he was in some other place and jest saw them when we's getting to Santiago del Estero, and it was already too late.

We lacked helpers to sew those rags. The government, like always, turned a deaf ear when the Tucuman sent in an order for blue fabric for uniforms. How were they going to send us fabric if they didn't give us any food! I'm not exaggerating that by that time many of our boys weren't dying from the Barbarians' bullets as much as from plain hunger and weakness. I'm telling you, since I was in charge of cooking in these empty casseroles, tired of watery broths. If it hadn't of been for the good will of the people of the provinces who gave us what little bit they had, I don't know how much longer we would've lasted.

Teresa and Antonia couldn't complain, since they even got husbands in the Army. At first I spent my time swatting away those bottle flies that were buzzing around them. Don't forget that the battalions of Black and Browns was sent to the north. All good people, but tending toward laughter and more than willing to have a young woman who'd warm up their blood. But they respected me and with jest a look they quieted down. Now, if a girl was fetching, she prob'ly made out fine all by herself. For those needs we all do the impossible... Why, I sure know about that...

Now that my Sir Genrul is deceased, I'm prompted to tell you a secret: What I felt for him I have not felt ever for anybody.

Yes, I know what you're trying to tell me, I can divine it in that mischievous face. But I swear to you that what happened to me with him...

The one who pulled out of the air that something was up was that jealous, pushy Tucuman, who I went to the river with from time to time. Don't play the fool. You know what for. He liked being with us so much that I suspect he was a bit black himself.

But this one, the Goldilocks, he was my true Manuel. I learned it when I saw him for the first time, around when the English came into Buenos Aires. He went by, handsome like I always dreamed him, I swear to you. Blond, a sun, he appeared to be that saint Miss Eloísa had in her prayer book. Sakes alive, why didn't Obatalá make us more alike? Why it was a joke that he was so white and I was so black... Yah, I know that, before, I had another Manuel, but he was jest my husband, the father of my children. This was my love. In case you didn't know, for a woman those are mighty different things. She lives with one, for the other she gives her life. My Sir Genrul warmed my heart so much in those days. What happened between the two of us, whoever isn't dumb already knows.

Did I already tell you that death conquered all of my loved ones? For that reason it made me so mad to suspect that the Tucuman, the one I gave much pleasure to, dragged secrets out of me on purpose. I cannot swear it on the Virgin, but I suspect that he used my yuyos and my secrets to harm the other one. Because, if you think a bit, since I cured everybody, why could I not even drive out Goldilocks' pain from him? Since at the end, they were both more trusting, and they weren't like cats and dogs, he probably took advantage to give him some trash. I don't know, don't pay no attention to me, an old woman can be mean out of sheer laziness.

Who knows if I will have anyone when I leave this world. I hope it's quick. I don't have anything to do and I can barely get out of this hammock. If my boys should see me now, my Sir Genrul, what an embarrassment. Look at the broke-down mess I've become. Better you should remember me as Auntie María, as the Capitana of the old times.

EIGHT

When it comes to the dead, there's no recourse

Meaning to bring people to life with words, I began to torment María with a continuous parade of the living and the dead. Poor Bernardo; my mother, an Indian but redeemed; Ignacio, a coward but saved; my father, dead but alive, his obese widow, his two stupid daughters; Inés, the cook of the cradling embrace and the aroma of cumin, mistress of savory turnovers.

"God willing, she won't have died, María. She will teach you how people eat in Tucumán."

When we arrived at the stagecoach stop at Talachocha, I could no longer control my trembling. Trying to rein in so many anxieties, I plunged my head into a bucketful of water just pulled up out of the well. Something calmed me, but it is much easier to face up to the living, believe me. When it comes to the dead, there's no recourse.

The 18th of March in 1812 we arrived in Tucumán, where we stayed a few days before going on to Yatasto.

No one passes through the land of my birth, hot and boisterous like its people, without falling in love with it. Carolina poplars, pepper trees, bamboo, oranges, and palms make it more akin to Lima than to Salta or Jujuy.

At the entrance to the city, bunches of dirty little barefoot children were waiting for us, and they ran along hanging onto our horses with grins and fresh water, convinced that with our arrival their privations would come to an end.

Memories treacherously attacked me, and they mingled with the flavor of tears, the ones you do not cry—the worst kind because they remain inside and make your emotions turbulent enough to set you loose among the memories.

Without giving any explanations (no one asked for any), I pulled out from the widest part of the column, and I got home with my heart galloping like my horse.

Everything there stood on the dark side of my memories. This time, only a solitary Bernardo awaited me, alerted to my coming by a letter I had sent him from Rosario. He waited for me in the doorway. The burden of his unprotected state hunched his back, and he had aged as in death.

What he gave me was not an embrace. Shipwrecked in the middle of the storm, he clung to me; his hug squeezing off my breath. He started to sob desperately. I did too, feeling that remorse, with its usual power, had come back for a visit. In truth I had forgotten how weak, how vulnerable this brother of mine was, this orphan of life.

In the house everything was the same and yet so different. The death of her husband had made it possible for the obese widow, who even in pain could not lose any weight, to give free rein to her baroque instincts that only my father's Hispanic frugality had kept in check. Damask curtains of crimson silk, chairs of calfskin embossed with incredible designs, silver incense holders where Peruvian incense burned, making the air more rarefied, mirrors with golden frames from which hung grapes by the bunch and stupid chubby angels, all had invaded the serenity of the rooms. It was no longer my home.

I paid my respects to that corseted, distant Rivas, who was irritated by my presence. I would deal with her later.

The outbursts of my black nursemaid Inés broke the silence as weighty as a reproach and, before I knew it, I was enveloped in that humanity smelling of thyme, mint, and vanilla. She gave me all her love through her cooking.

"At last, Chile Gregorio, at last! If you'd delayed a single day more, Chile, Bernardo would've died on us."

And I believed her.

The first rays of the sun the following morning were accusation against Bernardo and me sitting in the back patio, completely inebriated with spirits, melancholy, and love, in equal parts. We drank to the health of Father Ignacio, on whose health we also shat now and again, with shouts so loud that I am sure he heard them in Rome.

The one who heard us for certain was Inés, and as if we were still the children she had raised, she took us each by an arm to bed where for twelve hours straight we slept off the binge of our reunion, in each other's embrace.

The short stroll I took the next afternoon revealed to me that nothing was the same in my hometown, and even less so with the noisy, demanding presence of the army. For Tucumanos, that was a group of conceited Porteños disrupting their lives.

In Tucumán, as in the rest of the Northern provinces, loyalties were as mixed up as the blood of Spaniards and Creoles. No one had a clear plan for the Revolution, and that was not good.

Hostility came from the most humble people, the ones who go from being poor to being even poorer. The other ones, the people who realized that the North was the gateway for the Barbarians, already in the Humahuaca gorge, knew that blood would inevitably flow.

Since around the last stagecoach stop before Tucumán, I had already seen the sorry one-horse outfits where misery reigned. They were places without men, since they had been taken by force to serve the country, henceforth to become deserters. They had left behind them unsown plots, scrawny harvests yet to be picked, and children starving to death. That is how poverty settled in at the North and, as is known, revolutionary ideals become ever more distant and ridiculous on an empty stomach.

The depressed spirit of those years was notable, even in Tucumán's social life where, before, anything was cause for a party. In other times, San Miguel Archangel, patron of the city, or San Benito, patron of the blacks, were celebrated with pagan joy. Three days of fireworks, public dances, discussion groups, rum, grain alcohol, ring games, and concupiscence left the city exhausted and happy. Now all of that had fallen into oblivion.

But, despite the dejection, a persistent hope grew after our arrival. Young men of all social classes had been ready since the year before to join the army, with parental consent or not. Hundreds of men and women—artisans, tradesmen, and farmers—contributed whatever they could. Chickens, saddles, ponchos, medicines, jerky, alcohol, candles, and soap, all of it began to move by itself into hearts and onto backs and carts, which in the camp became jumbled up in an anarchic pile that we all refused to organize.

The night before beginning the march toward Campo Santo, the governor, Domingo García, threw a dance and party for the officers. In a time without joy, he could not pass up such an excellent opportunity for a festivity.

The dance enlivened the spirits of everyone in the city; it gave a blush to married women and hope to maidens. It obliged the officers to take a decent bath and the musicians to tune their instruments for polkas and minuets.

In the back patio, and in spite of my dear stepmother's fury at the invasion of noisy black women, María and her daughters, quickly intimates of Inés, mended, sewed, washed, and ironed uniforms and shirts for the officers who, having just bathed, cut across to the house without even noticing the presence of my swooning fat stepsisters.

As soon as I went out with Bernardo, reeking of flower water, the black women shoved the three Rivas into the carriage, so corseted that they could barely breathe, and then ran to get gussied up. Then they flew to the shindig, which promised them a thousand pleasures, after so much post-poned happiness.

The dance given by the governor brought together all the respectable people in the city, who circled Belgrano as soon as he arrived, stepping on each other to be introduced.

Dressed-up to the point of extravagance, he caused the women's eyes to roll back in their heads and the men to bow from the waist in reverence.

Introductions, hand-kissing, greetings, and smiles. All of a sudden Bernardo, his betrothed, the general, and I found ourselves in a circle of deadly silence that no one broke. Without knowing it, that night at the party, luck set us all up for its first trick. Obliged by the situation, Bernardo made the introductions. Dolores Helguera was truly as beautiful as he had told me in his letters. Just a girl, but behind the look in her hazel eyes was the character that was lacking in my brother.

"General, may I present Miss Dolores Helguera, my fiancée," my brother said, in a voice bursting with pride.

The amount of time they stood looking at each other was long enough to foretell misfortune.

The guest of honor had the first dance with the governor's wife, who, sweating like a cart-driver, did not get a single step right during the entire piece. With a bow he freed himself from her and, crossing the hall, approached Dolores.

"Bernardo, allow your betrothed to save me from continuing to dance with the First Lady," murmured Belgrano, looking only at her.

My brother accepted with pleasure, not suspecting that in that instant she was being taken from him forever. It always angered me about life that it did not wink, or give a signal, an alarm, something to alert us to the precise moment when a careless action of ours became a turning-point and forever made a bend in our path. But no matter, it gives no warning, and with the perspective of years, one just now discovers the destiny that hid itself in an instant that should never have been.

Dolores wore a light pink dress, her hair pulled back in a bun, and, as adornment, a simple pearl necklace; in reality she needed nothing more. She looked with adoring eyes at Belgrano, and both whirled, whirled, and whirled, far away, far far away *the snot-nose doesn't take her eyes off of you and*

Bernardo doesn't even realize he wants to swallow you with his look if he keeps on looking like that I'm capable of hitting you you shitty snot-nose at your side Bernardo seems like a dimwit with that face of loving happiness just about girls nothing more they're all snakes not all not you my negrita you're the most trustworthy person I've ever known in my life I always know what you're thinking with that willingness you always have for love so as to not seem entranced why, you spent the night kissing hands and bowing it's no matter you were born for the ballroom I don't like this at all this Dolores for sure she'd get undressed if you asked her to but she can sit waiting since you're not going to ask her.

The women gossiped happily as in the old days. Drooling over the fair general with such refined manners, almost a Frenchman, they looked with scorn at their lackluster spouses, who hid yawns after an exhausting day of work.

The crystal chandeliers let teardrop decorations break up the candlelight into a thousand shards that like darts lit up the room, transforming it into a painting of the French school. I hurried over to one side and, taking up a spectator's position, looked upon the scene, obliging myself to sketch every detail. The officers who wore the girls out with vigorous dance steps, the old men who, already tipsy, told each other off-color jokes, the matrons who crossed their fingers so their daughters would trap some eligible man, the old women who, believing no one saw them, opened their evening bags to hide small cakes, tomorrow's squashed breakfast. The girls who had not yet been asked to dance sent messages to eligible boys with their fans: open was "yes," slowly touching each rib was "I don't trust myself," closed was "no," the index finger softly along the side was "we have to talk." More than intuiting it, I knew that I was observing one of the last festivities I would attend in my life. Given that absolute certainty, I dedicated myself to completely enjoying the party.

The next morning, my eyes bloodshot from the liquor and the long night, I bade Bernardo goodbye until the following week when, without any further procrastinations, I would return to sit down with him and the account books in order to inventory the goods that would become part of the estate.

While I approached my mount with a sackful of jerky, sweets, and warm tortillas, Inés whispered to me: "Take care, Chil' Gregorio, she's a daughter of Olorúm. She's not any ole black woman. She's sacred. Don't you go looking at her that way. She's sacred."

The black woman's voice broke with those warnings. My hearty laugh infuriated her. "You'll see. Don't believe me, but you're going to see..."

I needed to silence the truth. I had not just looked at her "like that," as Inés naïvely prohibited me from doing. Kumbá, the sacred one, was mine. I had crossed all the paths of her body, to the extent that I only fell short of making love to her shadow, but I would do that too.

What we found on our arrival at Yatatso could not be considered an army. It was a pathetic group of men beaten down in Huaqui by a strong, powerful enemy. Skinny, sickly, in pain, malnourished, dressed in rags, the majority could barely stand up. They had no weapons, food, or spirit. Given our commander's state of health, and with these troops, we were not going to be able to withstand even a day's march. I could not help laughing. If the enemy saw us, he would not attack out of pity, pure and simple.

But once again, and much to my sorrow, I was going to witness that singular alchemy that took place each time Belgrano came in contact with his men. He called them together in such a way that his mere presence brought even the wounded to their feet and, in his first words of greeting, he already managed that those dregs, who might be dead the next day, would shout a delirious "Viva la Patria!" And I painfully discovered, despite all my efforts to keep him from it, that he was indeed making History.

The time had come for her to go on alone

The time was approaching when María Kumbá would start being on her own. It was also in June, this time in 1807, when the English, blinded by their never-ending greed, disembarked for the second time in the Bay of Barragán.

Since the year before, people had been organized into militias under Liniers' command. And María was proud to be the wife of a soldier in the Black and Browns battalion.

During the long macumba the night before in El Tambor Mayor, the city's blacks began their offerings. Standing upright in the center of a star drawn in the hard-packed dirt, she called to her Orishá warriors. There, like the corolla of a supplicant flower, she raised her arms upward, and the gods took possession of her, whispering news of the victory. The price would be very high, but they would crush those colorless strangers who spoke an incomprehensible language.

That morning María bade her husband goodbye with a longer embrace than usual, knowing without knowing that it would be the last, and then she ran to the big house of her childhood, to defend the country from there.

The master greeted her with a silence full of looks. No explanations were necessary. And despite the fact that one day she had rejected the white part of herself, it moved her to perceive in the man's eyes something like pride. Given her aloofness, she would continue to resemble him more than anyone of her race.

The house was a beehive of nervous preparations and everyone carried to the balcony whatever would serve as a projectile to use against the invader. As in the rest of the city, the big house was made into a fortress. Buenos Aires had the premonition that the final battle would be waged in its bowels, in the veins of its streets. Behind the heavy doors of the houses, the whole town was poised in tense expectation, while the smell of death spread slowly, in compliance with the Orishá's prediction.

Oh, Santa María! What fury your children used to defend you! Gun smoke mixed with the smoke that arose from burned enemy flesh, made into chittlins by the shower of boiling grease and oil that fell in copious streams of death from the rooftops.

The battle exacted a high price for each American life. The blond invaders were the targets of rocks, sticks, wagon wheels, and mortars that all fell down from the balconies.

And one day, in the midst of the fighting, when she hurriedly opened the front door for the servant who brought news of what was happening in the barrios, she saw him. It was him! Before her was the face of the man who had long been an inhabitant of her dreams. The person she had been destined for had entered her life, the person she would accompany in battles and in death. He passed by at the head of a group of disorderly men, looking straight ahead, his clothes dirty and soaked in sweat. He tried to find the order he was used to in the midst of so much disorder among those common people, a disorder that he would have to become accustomed to.

After three days of fighting, dirty and beaten-down by fatigue, María began to hear the voices of the Orishás who whispered gloomy news to her. They had annihilated the invader, but now they would know the cost of the victory. Terrified, hopping over all the bodies indistinctly jumbled-up together, she went in search of her husband, the anonymous black Manuel. The gods guided her to San Telmo, and in a corner she found the wide-eyed cadaver of her husband, looking sweetly into the infinite.

Her daughters, who had followed without her knowing it, embraced the body of their father, with all the pain of having lost their beginning. On her feet, but dizzy with grief, María's visions became crossed, and she was her grandmother in far-off Africa, standing before the body of her man, who had fallen defending his own.

Where was it written that through her veins should always flow the blood of the victims? You fell, Black Manuel, in some old corner of a city that never took notice of your death.

And though she embraced him, trying to fill him with life, he didn't wake up. The time when she was to go on alone was definitely coming. Of course the future frightened her. Freedom is always frightening, but when it comes, it stays forever.

Buenos Aires wasn't generous with the blacks and mulattoes who fought for it. Whites couldn't find the loyalty to comply with their promise to free the bravest ones. Perhaps, because having done so, there would have been no more slaves. Instead, Buenos Aires made into an indignant game of chance the freedom of a handful, compared to the hundreds who cursed their servitude.

That day, along the front of the main plaza, almost seven hundred slaves lined up, trembling with the anticipation of freedom, their names on slips of paper placed in an indifferent urn. It would only spit out seventy freed men, who were embarrassed to savor their freedom as they faced their luckless brothers.

Nor did those of black blood merit the fear Buenos Aires felt knowing that they and the mulattoes of the city were armed. The government stipulated a reward for those who turned in their weapons, which sounded like a slap in the face. There was no need for such egotism in the face of such courage, in the face of so much spilt blood.

María Kumbá buried her husband in the gloomy cemetery of the Convent of San Francisco and was now alone with her girls to confront life. But anyone with clear vision, could see Shangó at her side guiding her steps toward the destiny that had been fixed for her that melancholy autumn of her birth.

**Oshún, mother of the most indulgent,
she who possesses enormous, robust breasts,
she who calms children, she who offers
curative waters in exchange for nothing at all,
she who is not flesh and blood. Save me!**

Don't go being confused on account of seeing me quiet here in this hammock. Though you mightn't believe me, in the barrio, for Carnival, when the Dance of the Kings or San Juan was put together, or for Christmas, I was the first one to organize the celebration.

Any old reason worked for going dancing and singing. That's how grief and pain go away, upset by the commotion the music makes. When we set to dancing in the midst of the procession for San Baltasar or San Benito, the priests got furious. They said we was disrespectful. How can that be...? Why, the saints are real happy to see people singing to them rather than looking down at the ground and burning their hands with the tallow the candles drip on them. The Orishás love it when people dance for them and sing to them, jest another way of praying. So, then they come down happier and they enter into the bodies of the dancers.

You might say I don't hold a grudge, and I don't have memories for bad things, but in those days we blacks suffered something fierce. Now things is going along somewhat better, and jest this year Juancito, my grandson, could go to school. During the times I'm telling you about, we broke our sweet backs, slaves and freed, from sunup to sundown. I don't know what was worse, to be a slave or go free with your belly empty.

Back in the day, when it wasn't even turning light, I used to jump out of bed, still nighttime, and go hurrying off to the slaughterhouse. I had to hurry because bunches of folks shoved through the doors to be the first to grab what was left over after the carving. The butchers was already selling the scraps and guts, and that's all we had money for. The feet and the blood they gave to the black beggars or the sickly, for soup at least. When it was mighty hot, from a distance, a body would get dizzy from the rotten smell. You can't begin to know the size of those green flies that flew over the dead beef animals full of blood, their bellies cut open and the guts hanging out. You walked slipping and sliding in the purple mud puddles made by dirt and blood. But it wasn't so bad. When we got fresh intestines with good color, we'd braid them before putting them on the grill. That's the best way to cook them, excepting the curlicues by themselves fall onto the coals, while the braided ones get grilled jest right, crispy. Don't force me to remember 'cause it makes my mouth water.

The question is to find a knack for things and to put on a good face. Who told you that the rich are happier. I'm going to tell you so's you know. Years later when I returned to the big house to defend the city against the English, I saw Marsis Eloísa again. We were brought up together. She was even my half-sister, you already know from where... When I went up to her to give her greetings, she didn't even recognize me. Truth is that neither did I. She was so washed-out, wearing a black dress with a big old cross that hung from her neck; had a rosary in her hand and passed the time moving her lips, must've been praying. Crazy as a loon, the poor thing.

By and by, the cook told me that she'd not married and that the only beau she had vanished in thin air one fine day, and she stayed a little touched, with her trousseau ready, spying out the window of the parlor all the day long waiting for that bandit to return. And you see, so rich and so unhappy... You are not going to tell me that all the money in that family served some purpose for her.

You noticed how quiet the night is? Or could it be that on top of being old, I'm deaf? Before I used to like to stay in this hammock for the pure pleasure of listening to the crickets and remembering my dearly departed. But tonight I don't hear a sound. Even the bugs seem like they've gone to sleep. I reckon I'm alone in the world. What luck that I have this attentive young man calling on me. Why it even seems that I've known him all my life. He's got a familiar face... I'm not flattering you, young man. You're so kind to keep me company that it pains me to not be able to get up to steep you some maté. I'm worse than ever...

But, more alone than tonight, I did surely feel the day Mama Basilia died. Of a sudden, we came to be a shoal of orphans, because for all the Nagó people, she was our mother, our Babalawo. Yes, I know that she'd prepared me to take her place, and the poor soul was so wrinkled-up it tried your heart jest to look at her. But as much as you might suspect that death's circling the ones a body loves, when the time comes, all that suspicioning doesn't help. The afternoon she passed on, she was in the Sala, ready to see the first of her clients. I went up to her with a hunch of the worst on account of I saw her awful quiet, sitting with the seeds and the necklaces for consulting Ifá in her hand, not letting go of them. And jest before touching her I realized she had stole away with him. He'd come seeking her and had carried her off to repose with the Orishás who'd been her companions for so long. I won't tell you I was sad. It was awhile she'd been calling for them and she'd jest given herself the pleasure. But I swear to you that all of a sudden a loneliness so great came over me that my legs wouldn't hold me up. That happens when, from being so leisurely and trusting, you lean on a person so much that when the person passes on it seems like she takes your life. I embraced her like I did that time with my mama, but I didn't sing for her to return. I'd already learned that it doesn't work. I called to the Tatas Brujos and we had jest covered her face with a white silk cloth when I began to shake. I felt a mighty strong warmth that entered me through my head and it continued till it left me without a breath, and right there I passed out. When I came to, I knew that the spirit of Mama Basilia had got into my body forever and they both were keeping Shangó company.

You can't imagine what the funeral was like. It lasted two whole days. The Babalawos from all the nations came, and the adjás and the drums didn't cease beating their farewell to her, like to a queen. That's what she was for us.

And that's when the trouble descended on me because they all saw me as the new Babalawo. And me not knowing how to tell them that I had to follow my Sir Genrul, that the Orishás ordered me to do that. Don't you laugh. I would've liked to see you in my shoes.

Thanks be to the little Virgin del Rosario, who never failed me, I was able to do the two things. Whilst I was in the barrio, I played Mama Basilia and, when it was my turn to fight, one of the Tatas Brujos of the Bantú nation attended to my people. They came from all over to the Sala. Bigwigs, sickly misses, and lovesick señoritas. Nobody went away complaining about my work, and they always returned or sent more folks. They didn't realize that half of the work they did themselves by believing in me. Lovesickness is the easiest to cure because Orishás always takes pity on the tears of girls in love. Look here, I'll tell you a secret: to get the love of some shameless fool, or make him come back to you, you first have to tie up three peacock feathers with a yellow silk ribbon and put them between your petticoats. Wear them for three days and on the morning of the fourth day, go secretly to the banks of a river, find a well-hidden black stone, and leave the Orishá an offering of honey, cinnamon, and eggs so he'll be content, because he's a real hungry glutton. Then you say: "My mother's house is the all-powerful river. Women who flee in search of salvation visit it often."

If that lover doesn't come back, for certain a better one will appear. I was so sought after for lovesickness that at times I had to shoo them off so's they'd allow me to attend to the truly sick ones.

When I was to be joining couples together and making the dying healthy I learned the time had come nigh to go with my Sir Genrul to Paraguay. Mama Basilia had told me.

Ha! Made me laugh, the fussing of a few I better not name when they found out that he'd been elected to head up the expedition. They cussed saying they didn't understand why they'd elected a halfway touched little Bible-beating lawyer. And they was never going to understand it. You know why? Because they never asked me...

NINE

It is not worth it to ask life for quarter, as it gives none

We set up our General Headquarters in Campo Santo, an advance outpost for Salta. Look where you would, there was disorder everywhere. How to begin to shape into an army a handful of men, beasts, and weapons that time and defeat had rendered useless? They stained the landscape with so much accumulated pain.

They were the survivors of the massacre at Huaqui. Months back they had come down from the Upper Peru in a chaotic retreat. Animals and men descended to escape from a certain Goyeneche who sought to crush them. Though the locals pleaded with them not to abandon them to the Spanish and their vengeance, the army of Porteños did not stop. They leveled hamlets in search of food, and each one watched out for his own hide. Pueyrredón, their commander, was the one who set the example. In a sudden outburst of altruism, he decided to liberate the treasure in the Treasury House in Potosí, and without a moment's doubt carted off all the gold and silver that was there. But, mysteriously, the mule that carried the treasure box with the gold disappeared on the journey, and he too, mysteriously, also fell ill. Despised and cursed by his men, he declared himself to be on the verge of death and asked to be relieved, despite the healthy color in his cheeks. The golden reasons he obviously reserved for himself. And that is how he left the Upper Peru completely unprotected and bankrupt.

Men: Fifteen hundred

Rifle cartridges: Thirty thousand

This is how to begin a simple inventory of the army that was to face five thousand well-armed Spaniards.

The suffering humanity of those dejected soldiers yanked me out of my ironic guise of mere spectator. More than four hundred sick and wounded abandoned to their fate, laid out on the bare ground and wrapped in threadbare blankets was a difficult spectacle to contemplate. The smell of blood, urine, and human excrement was unbearable. Cuts, crawling with worms their owners plucked out with their fingers, soon became wounds before the impotent gaze of doctors who did not know how to multiply their science.

They ate when some kindly neighbor woman approached them with a skimpy ration snuck out behind her husband's back. The misery of that Porteño army that had been pillaging them for two years no longer moved the men of the North, who were fed up with their messianic declarations of freedom.

In life-and-death situations, one tends to react with extreme attitudes, and so, in a display of patriotism that left even me surprised, I informed Manuel Belgrano that I would take charge of the correspondence to request the necessary assistance for our helplessness.

As I was in my home territory, I moved with the ease of a Rivas, and the prominent families who lived off mine did not turn a deaf ear. This was not being asked of them by a Porteño military man who intended to continue with the plundering and looting they were accustomed to since the Castelli era. The one asking them was an equal who persuaded them that this time the army would not abandon them.

That way I could begin stockpiling the medicines that until then were as completely unknown to me as they were indispensable to the infirm. Powdered quinine, stalks of quinine, sulfur buds, saltpeter, ceruse, stickywilly, mustard plaster, corrosive sublimate, lead acetate, needles for suturing, materials for surgery, and hundreds of pieces of linen for bandages began to arrive from places nearby and some not so close, raising the hopes of the wounded men and filling the empty medicine kits.

With the success of seeing the moribund of the night before standing up by the next midday, I almost felt myself to be a god, and drunk with my omnipotence, I claimed more power. The restocking of uniforms and cavalry equipment quickly came under my control.

I returned to my task of epistolary requests, putting to the test the generosity of the Tucumanos, Salteños, Jujeños, to whom I gave my word, in flashes of wit, that they would never again be humiliated by the Porteños.

But little could we trust Buenos Aires, that sent its worst ambassadors to strip the provincials of their public offices, leaving them on the street. Occupied in disputing power amongst themselves, the people of Buenos Aires could not heed the suffering of a distant people who lived on remote frontiers. They never smelled dung, or blood. They never heard the screams of the dying, nor saw arms and legs at a remove from their owners.

I continued with my task of collecting money and good will, and next came the moment for uniforms. Once the bolts of blue fabric arrive, the hundreds of stays, of material for lining, of baize, cashmere, and darning yarn for shirts, thread, whalebone buttons, insignias, scissors and thimbles, I commissioned a group of twelve operators and three master tailors with the making of pantaloons, jackets, shirts, capes, bow ties, and caps. They were overseen by María and her daughters, who piled up the clothing and classified it as it came out of the shop that we improvised south of the campground.

Empty at night, the place was inhabited by our nocturnal encounters. We did not have all the time in the world, as at Paraná, and in the brief escapades we permitted ourselves, we frolicked happily between the mounds of fabric, letting flesh take charge of life. Our bodies had become accustomed one to the other to such an extent that the mere wait of another minute made our hands shake with the rush to undress each other. We avidly inhaled each other's scent and only then could we go on living.

Making footwear turned out to be not so easy. Most of the men had never worn shoes and their feet, deformed by that freedom, could only take shoes made with a soft sole instead of one made of cordovan. The master shoemakers needed to widen their lasts, and discarding frugality, they rounded the tips of the footwear to the point of exaggeration.

Cantles, saddle blankets, cinches, pallets, stirrups, spurs, bits, reins, saddles, and fur-lined pads were rigorously inventoried and delivered to the stable hands and carriage boys, who were under penalty of being shot if anything was lost. María followed me around sticking her nose in everything. My mood determined whether to accept her help or not. Most of the time I accepted her proximity, though for nothing more than smelling her aroma. She was happy to feel useful, and her songs could be heard in the camp at any time.

In spite of some initial stumbles, I was soon able to report that the reorganization of the munitions depot and artillery park, and likewise the tailoring of uniforms, were complete.

Indifferent to the heat and my successes, Belgrano inspected the camp day and night, taking charge of the most minimal details: food for the sick, who kept on dying right before our eyes; the manufacture of cartridges; the training of recruits, who cried at night; the organization of a Disciplinary Tribunal that would later have deserters shot without mercy. Putting its parts together, he coaxed that disarticulated giant up onto its feet. That delirious activity earned him the mockery of soldiers who laughed behind his back and whispered. "Annoying brat," or "the nation's dummy" were some of the nicknames that went from mouth to mouth, giving rise to stifled laughs *but just the same they begin to respect you damn where do I put all this hatred that gets blocked up in me, that I can't share with anybody sometimes with Dorrego but only sometimes because he hates you so much he doesn't want to talk about you my little mulatto you don't want to hear my anger either I lost the chance to have you removed from your post you continue as the head of the army and now with a thirst for vengeance that makes you crazy better for me that way the mistakes won't delay in coming.*

The people's hatred of that distant revolution did not help, and a thousand times over they preferred the familiar proximity of the Spanish who were, in fact, neighbors, parents, friends.

Given the apocalyptic news that the government pen-pushers would send us not one single rifle, the arrival of a German adventurer to the camp was taken to be a miracle. He called himself the Baron de Holmberg, and only Belgrano succumbed to the exaggerated weight of that title. He was European nobility, according to himself. From my point of view, he was a sponger, an impenitent sinner who for a few pesos the army paid out, unveiled all his science, truly close to an art, and in a short time he had completed the founding of four bronze culverins and a good number of pieces of heavy artillery.

Ominous news began to come down from the North. Cochabamba had fallen, and with it, the last resistance in the Upper Peru. They say it was defended to the end by their heroic women when they were faced with the lukewarm courage of the men, who preferred surrender. And hundreds of women died, between pillaging and rape in the streets of the city, at the hands of an army of Porteños that in 1810 had incited the region to take up arms. Now, the terrified emissaries came to warn us that the well-provisioned enemy was moving easily down the Humahuaca Gorge, closer by the day.

August arrived. It is the month of bad luck and worse death, since diabolic spirits walk around unfettered, searching for the tired souls of sick people to carry off.

The reality was ever more alarming. The Barbarians came so close that we took six men prisoner from a forward guard sent to spy on us. We barely had time to break camp, hide the sick and wounded in nearby rundown ranches, and start a quick, rag-tag retreat safeguarding the families of Jujuy who had emigrated with us.

Days before, without consulting anyone, Belgrano made a frightening public announcement that the population of Jujuy had to abandon their homes, poison the water in their wells, and hide their cattle and their harvests. The enemy had to find loneliness and destruction in his path. He would find himself in the middle of nowhere with no food. I ask myself to this day if such a sacrifice was necessary.

The populace left cursing, less than meek in their obedience. Seed beds destroyed, water courses broken down, houses abandoned, were all the very high price they had to pay for a freedom they had not asked for. They were only able to save their public records to not lose their memory, and liturgical objects to not lose their faith.

Belgrano, reviving Moses, reclaimed a blind acceptance of law. "He who does not obey will be executed," he announced without remorse, in a hurry to set the columns in motion.

María and her daughters, multiplied to infinity, arranged with the women of Jujuy for the transportation of the children, the aged, and the sick in the few wagons and carriages that they were permitted to redirect to that end. Thus, among malodorous hides and dirty cleaning rags, three women gave birth during the march. It is not worth it to ask life for quarter, as it gives none. The lack of order, the clouds of dust, our fears, and the enemy rolled over us, civilians, military, women, and children.

We marched on day and night, so close together that our

rear guard clashed in a permanent skirmish with the Barbarians' advance guard. Our tail, their head; given so much proximity league after league of pursuit, they had fraternized and began to exchange cigars, coca leaves, pieces of jerky, and obscene jokes.

The smoke from the hayfields that are burned off in August to scare away spirits and improve the land also served to cover us. Slaughtered cattle were strewn along the road, their eyes open, their stiff legs begging for pity from heaven, and their flesh rotted, with no time to make it into jerky. Piled up with the history of a family, carriages with broken axles were abandoned to the flames so they would not be violated by enemy hands.

With great suffering we came to the banks of the pitifully dry Piedras river, where we left all the women and children in the rear guard, and improvised a ferocious defense with the fury that dispossession grants. Common laborers, soldiers, tradesmen, gauchos, priests, matrons and children, all took part in that battle. By four o'clock in the afternoon we had routed the enemy and we rested, drunk with our victory. But the government sent strict orders to continue on toward the south without fighting.

We had heated discussions that lasted until dawn, and the words, hardened by sleep and fatigue, remained in our mouths. To move south meant ceding the territory we had won at a very high price.

Our neighbors in Jujuy, Salta, and Tucumán, already aware of the fierce enemy descending from the north, yelled out warnings that we had to stop them right away. And to my satisfaction, they were furious in threatening Belgrano, advising him that, if he left them unprotected, they would not collaborate with the army, and they themselves would become enemies. The time had come, they said, to be compensated for all past humiliations. And, of course, we disobeyed, with great pleasure. We laconically informed Buenos Aires that, were we to heed the orders, we would lose the provinces of the North, and that is how we sent those orders to hell and damnation.

Our insubordination was proverbial. On account of it came the victories in Tucumán and Salta.

It was decided to wait for the Barbarians in my province. Money magically appeared, and volunteers also. In three days, six hundred gauchos were recruited. The Spanish neighbors who lived within twenty leagues of Tucumán were locked up, in case their allegiances might betray them in some unguarded moment.

My city's valor filled me with pride. Belgrano looked with fright at the gauchos, those simple, savage men who noisily presented themselves to offer their lives. They must have tapped into all his energy, since their happy, odiferous presence began to relax the infamous discipline based on arrests and jailings *the same nauseated face for the blacks you put on now for the gauchos gratitude doesn't come from you upon seeing that they leave all or nothing to fight without asking for anything and though it annoys you they holler because they're happy they make noise because they're alive gauchos blacks Indians you look down on them you say that your dream of America isn't for us you get upset they're undisciplined what the hell does it matter to you that they don't know how to come to orderly formation if they put their shoulders to it and defend the land of their ancestors what do you know about land and ancestors if you were always a demoted baron duke prince that you would really have liked to be you got screwed and were born here and here the crowns were the ones the Indians had until they were taken away from them my great-grandfather took one and they whipped him to death but you're not going to be able to avoid it this land will be ours the ones who fight for it and win it will keep it.*

María, who was in an excellent frame of mind regarding her Sir Genrul's health, had to use all her authority in order to keep the people of Tucumán from taking apart the convoy of foodstuffs she guarded with her life. And it was her rolling pin that in the end convinced those wild gauchos that no one played around with her.

Victory came back to us and the bells of my home town tolled for hours celebrating our feat. In large measure, we owed it to the somewhat unorthodox attack by our gauchos. Armed with pikes, lances, daggers, and boleadoras, howling like the damned in the midst of the noise of their leathers and the swirling of their ponchos, they paralyzed the enemy with terror when they were faced with those gauchos who seemed to be sent from hell itself.

The victory gained by disobeying instructions from Buenos Aires confirmed our leadership, the leadership of those who risk their lives for ideals, diffuse yet foreseen.

The 25th of May arrived

On her daily trip to the river with her washtub of dirty clothes, she once heard sonorous words that rhymed together as if they weren't aware of it. LIBERTY, EQUALITY, FRATERNITY. They were pronounced secretly, under the breath, in a ring of young people, passionate dreamers who savored them with coffee, full of devotion, laden with the future. To María their musical sound seemed perfect, and while she pounded the clothes with a club trying to get them white, she put a music of her own invention to the words and moved to the beat of a secret melody. Her cadenced voice caressed the three words that she arranged at her whim.

Everyone in El Tambor knew that she was the one to take Mama Basilia's place, and whoever needed for the gods to make their lives less painful, sought her out knowing that she would find the precise word, the appropriate potion, the correct Orishá for the ill that afflicted them. She accepted life and said goodbye to it with the same serene gaze, and for those of her race she was the sure link that held them to their African roots.

With what love her brothers looked at her, when they came afflicted, seeking relief, and went away brimming with hope! And she was for all of them the protecting shade that Yemoja sent to console them for the uprootedness and the slavery they were condemned to.

Her daily trips through the streets with her already well-known almond cookies allowed her to become familiar with the secret societies that worked the town's underground threads, the threads that would go on knitting the story that the month of May would give birth to a contradictory and indecisive nation.

And she was going through the streets hawking her wares when she saw her blonde Manuel once again. Once, twice, three times she passed by close to him, who was

117

untouchable, unreachable, lost in his world. And when she saw him she became paralyzed, and her life escaped from her body and Ifá had to come to shake her to give her back her pulse, because you couldn't simply die of proximity. And the angry Orishás whispered to her that Kumbá, their envoy, could not become faint-hearted in that way, scarcely months away from when they would begin their journey together. It was him, the visage of her dreams, the true Manuel. The mystic, crazy general who would attempt to carry out a task he was not prepared for, but that nonetheless had awaited him since time immemorial. The worlds he would move in, right and wrong, would be war, not reason, the army, not the embassy, but always, always guided by inner voices, relatives of her Orishás, who had also come down to his crib that melancholy morning in June.

In May of 1810 there was a change being prepared in which there wouldn't be bloodshed or violence. Those would come in quantity later on, and would fatally seal almost 50 years of history.

A sleepy plaza and a calm Town Hall would be the stage where the desires of the young, the dreams of visionaries, and the yearning of slaves would materialize. They all had their secret reasons to dream. Even the smugglers in cahoots with the English. And all those reasons also weighed in.

There will be a few notables who can't tolerate the idea of a fortified populace, and who will close the doors of their houses, scandalized by the laughter and voices that come from the plaza. And in front of their closed doors, the breeze of renovation will pass by without asking permission and break useless schemes. They will learn that a few can't put a brake on the passion for a future, which in the hands of a bunch of lunatics will leave nothing as it had been.

In the midst of the laughter of the sons of those worried ones who listened to the hubbub from behind their doors was María Kumbá, giving away her wares to those who hopped from one foot to the other in an effort to trick the damp cold of those days.

The profile of the Auntie María of Vilcapugio, and of Ayohuma, was already being drawn, the one who would protect so many of those who would later be sacrificed, up there in Upper Peru. Many of those same ones were in the Plaza.

The gods had already announced to her that the delivery wouldn't be easy, and it would use up her nights in secret ceremonies, pulsing to the beat of ignomo and lonjas drums that entreated Olorúm for the prompt advent of a new era.

The 25th of May arrived, and she was among those who waited for two days in front of the Town Hall, dripping with rain and the future. No one left the Plaza. Her throat was scratchy from singing out the wares that she ended up giving away. Invoking the Orishás, her voice mixed in with hundreds of voices, drawn together at the tolling of the bells, in a yell that greeted the first government that, on the strength of her prayers, included her fair Manuel.

The Orishás state that with our words we ought to never initiate problems or provoke conflicts. (One of the moral commandments of the Odú)

What a mistake my Sir Genrul made when he ordered the Patricians to cut their braids! I never forgot that he became mighty angry when something got in his way, stubborn like a mule. He liked for all of us to be really quick about minding him. I'm not saying he was bad, Heaven help me! But it could only occur to a hardhead like him that the Patricians would allow their braids to be cut without a peep. Imagine. It was his pride.

You can't know what a row got stirred up! The thousand men of the regiment locked themselves in the barracks and said no one entered or left until Sir Genrul was relieved of command. Outside, with all the clamor that was stirred up, onlookers began to gather. Wives yelled out pleading, with their husbands to please stop their foolishness and come out at once. They spent the whole day shouting at them to put a stop to the takeover, and to open the gates. But there was no response. The only thing they wanted was for Sir Genrul to go. The revolt was so great that the government lost its head and ordered those outside to go in shooting.

That sure enough was terrible, young man. Anybody at all could cross over into the middle of the shooting and the smoke, the cries of alarm and the shoving. They even killed a child playing near the main gate. She was the little girl of one of the Patricians inside. They shot her in the back, poor little thing. Lying on the ground with her dress full of blood was how her mother found her, and when she began to scream it made all the people even crazier, shoving to get inside.

After that disaster, the ones in the barracks surrendered, but it was already too late. The folks on the government side were so worked up that as a lesson they had ten of the leaders shot and they jailed a bunch more. They hung the dead ones in the street so everybody could see them. You don't do that. The dead are to be buried as they should be, so they can rest in peace. At the top of their voices, women cried for pity for their sons, husbands, or brothers, but nothing doing. They jest killed them like animals... And that whole mess my Sir Genrul kicked up all by himself out of the pure mule-headed he could get when he became angry. That fuss with the trial for the business of Paraguay lingered on. But he shouldn't have been so stubborn. What fault did those poor Patricians have, I ask you? He should've tangled with his buddies in the government who didn't defend him so good.

But other times being mule-headed gave him luck. Like at the North, with that curse of the gods called soroche *that can kill any human being without a qualm. When we were around Jujuy, chasing after the Barbarians, at those heights where the clouds get stuck in your eyes, most of them commence to drop like flies, throwing up green liquid that you don't know the source of 'cause they didn't have nothing in their bellies. Jest imagine. Those of us from Buenos Aires, how were we going to get used to those atrocious mountains that seemed like walls for being so tall! The wind started in the morning, rousing up so much dust that we couldn't breathe, and in the afternoon it kept on worse, whistling and moaning like a ghost. I swear to you it made you feel like crying real loud. And I'm not exaggerating one bit, young man, I swear. Put yourself in our place. We spent livelong days without eating or sleeping, our guts sounding out real pretty and our eyes closing by themselves from fatigue, and you had to continue on without letting up. The climb got harder 'n harder, but we didn't stop. Till we could no more. The altitude knocked us down jest like that, unannounced. It seemed our heads was goin' to burst and we didn't have the strength to even carry our weapons. What am I telling you about marching; why our legs seemed like logs. When we stopped to catch our breath, we didn't want to get up again. The lassitude was so great, I swear, that it looked like death.*

The Jujeños gave us leaves, the leaves of a plant from around there that we sucked on without swallowing. It was coca and you had to leave it in your mouth till it made a green wad. Truth told, it was magic. It woke you up and cleared your head. But pretty quick, on the ground again. And that's why I'm telling you that there it did us good that Sir Genrul happened to be so stubborn. When he saw how soroche *was killing us, he began to go column by column hollering at us to not give in, pushing us to not let up, reminding us that the same thing was happening to the enemy. What do you want me to say? Seeing Goldilocks up there mounted on his horse, with so much gumption, saying pretty things about the country and how important we were, it jest made you feel like going on.*

But me he couldn't fool. I'd seen him at night in a cold sweat and throwing up his guts from how sick the altitude made him. And as though nothing, the next day once again he was back to the yelling. Olorúm inhabited him, of that I'm certain.

The ones who gave you pleasure with how they walked, just like goats, was the Indians. 'Course they lived around there. How were they going to feel the altitude! They were fierce fighters, and the more we climbed, more Indians joined us. They went about half-naked, without feeling the cold, armed with sticks and slingshots and some lances that scared you even from a distance. My Sir Genrul made himself loved among them too and his fame traveled so far that, while going through Potosí, a cacique showed up who was from I don't remember where, and if my memory doesn't fail me, he was named Cumbay. Well, I'm telling you...turns out this Cumbay was like the king of a rich tribe, that lived somewhere in the Chaco.

They say he'd heard so much talk about Sir Genrul that he desired to make his acquaintance, and he and all his men joined up with us. That passel of Indians put the fear of God in you; with those warlocks standing straight up and not a hair on the rest of their bodies. They even carried poison arrows. They became such friends, him and the Goldilocks, that when they said goodbye he made him a gift of a uniform jest like his. Cumbay, so's not to be left behind, and so's it could be seen that he also wanted freedom and was happy with the Revolution, left him two thousand of his Indians to help us fight. Shoot, for all it helped us. Like flies they dropped, jest the same as us, there at Vilcapugio and Ayohuma... Personally, the Orishás had told me the blood was going to flow like a river, but I didn't want to end up being convinced. We were lured along by the victories at Salta and Tucumán so that we thought the good luck wasn't ever going to abandon us. Me, on account of doubts, I never let up pleading with Olorúm so he'd help us. He couldn't leave us unprotected jest then because we were so far off, so poor and sick, almost all of us. They'd already told us in Jujuy that the climb up was no joke, that to go through the Quebrada de Purmamarca we needed scouts, ponchos, and food. But my Sir Genrul didn't want to wait at all, and we continued on, climbing. Seems to me his God coudn't love him much, if he made him mess up something fierce.

There was no way out of it. The blood flowed jest like a river. The poor souls fighted to the last breath, but there wasn't much we could do, with so many officers dead and nobody to give orders for anything. Me and my daughters ran from here to there closing the eyes of one, cradling the head of another, giving water to another one over there. We didn't stop so's not to think about the fright, and the bullets passing by so close you could only hear whistles. The smoke got into our eyes and we walked stumbling around with so many bodies lying every which way. The worst was when those that was bleeding to death, and they're realizing they's dying, grabbed us by the hem of our dresses so we wouldn't leave, weeping like babies, the poor things! Right then and there I got on my knees again and covered him with kisses and said to him: "Oh son, my son, rest easy, hang on a little 'cause you're going get better...," till he was all quiet and dead, poor thing. Then I would run to another, who was jest there next to him screaming in pain. In a few jugs some women from around there had given us, we collected all the water there was nearby. First, we'd wet our own heads so's not to faint from the heat and the smoke of the cannons, and then we'd go about giving it out to the wounded that would shortly pass on.

The Barbarians had us trapped like rabbits, and we were bewildered by the firing from all sides. Why, it was to die from crying to see all that jumble of rocks red with blood and covered with dead bodies. Some were missing a leg, others an arm. I remember one of my boys, who wasn't done dying yet, looking around for his legs. What! From his belly down was one jumble of scarlet. Better to not make me remember. I'm already old, and it does me ill to think about those days. I wept enough. My tears lasted me for years. Now you tell me something about yourself. Open up your mouth; nobody gets ahead of you if you're silent, is that it?

TEN

Our time had come to an end

A month after the September 24th victory, we carried the Virgin de las Mercedes through the streets of the city in a stately procession of gratitude. God and I have been in agreement only a few times, but that was one of them. No one can be so distracted as to not recognize a miracle.

We arrived at the campground where the battle took place. You could still see large red stains at every step as the dirt had not been able to absorb so much blood.

While the priest angrily pressed us to sing lively, I thought about the night I had spent with María. It was a hot, humid space at dusk where we stretched out until we came to the conclusion that we had managed an almost perfect replica of happiness.

Then we saw the approach of a group of men covered with dust, lead by Belgrano. They were returning to the city after having gone in pursuit of Pío Tristán. Dirty and tired from so many days without sleep, they mingled with us who were expressing our gratitude for so many favors from heaven.

Belgrano dismounted and approached the image. He asked them to lower the Virgin's platform. He attached a silk cord to his commander's staff, and kneeling, placed it on the Virgin. The Lady General of our army was from Tucumán.

We stayed in the city long enough to continue refurbishing the Army, exultant after such a victory. Captured by patriotic and culinary fervor, the women devoted themselves to preparing us cold cuts, goat cheeses, jerky, and salted mutton for the times ahead. And, already aroused by the flames of both passions, and others they dared not confess, they took down their copper cauldrons and, in a libertarian, erotic extravaganza, began to prepare sweets: chayote, lime, squash, orange, and quince, and to adjust their petticoats and corsets so that clumsy, male fingers would not delay longer than necessary. The life of the brave soldiers must be sweetened, whatever the cost. The price was set by the desire of both parties.

That was a time of public and private splendor in Belgrano's life. Everyone was dying to attend on the victor of the September 24th battle, and to lionize him. He was the Sun King before whom all bowed and genuflected, and a night did not pass but he was invited to a soirée in the houses of the prominent citizens. No one can resist the smell of victory.

During those months I devoted all the time I could to Bernardo, compensating him for past and future abandonment. Business was going from bad to worse. Field hands, laborers, drovers, all had been recruited by force, or had voluntarily joined the ranks, and there was no one to bring in the harvest. The mule herds thinned out at an alarming rate, given the needs of the royalist troops, and the not-so-royal but equally needy, who did not pause to make off with them, aided by the shadows of moonless nights. It was insanity to continue to trade with Upper Peru. Only the route to Buenos Aires saved us from total ruin. Despite the enormous distance, the still-operating fifty-six-stage coach that stops all along the road from the port to Tucumán provided us with indispensable services, such as repairing the ruts and potholes, and supplying capable workmen for help with broken-down carriages, exhausted travelers, and dying animals. Bernardo and I both missed our father's iron will that neither of us had inherited. Nor was either one of us able to maintain that business we detested.

While he was still receiving demonstrations of unconditional support, Belgrano built a pretentiously slapdash, insultingly cheap hovel near the fort, in an attempt to display his spiritual austerity. But he was no fool, and he surrounded himself with whatever he needed in order to be as far as possible from the camp and its riffraff.

And the beginning of the end came. No one told me about it. I saw it. With my own eyes I saw it, one moonless night when in a fit I was heading to his hovel to ask him to clarify a rumor that was insidiously consuming me. I had been told, with some sarcasm, that during a supper at the Zabaleta house Belgrano spent not a single second apart from Dolores, who had obviously arrived without Bernardo. Of course the commentaries flowed with the wine and Bernardo was referred to as a cuckold.

A few meters from his house, I saw a small form open the door and leave in shadows, wrapped in a dark shawl. The figure quickly mounted a horse and galloped off into the night. Too small, and too chestnut-colored to be other than Dolores Helguera, my future sister-in-law. It could not be true, for my brother, or for me...

I fled from the place, stumbling. That night I went to Félix's café. A poet, a crazy friend who should console me, who had discovered so much all at once *enough I won't go on with this it's not my place I don't know where it is but not at your side you little blond betrayer not believing in a cause I don't understand I'm wearing myself out in this work of being a spy or scribe for whom I don't know or for what if Saavedra my only friend goes around hiding like a thief what am I doing in the Army? what am I doing in Tucumán? I'm fed up with being transparent do I exist? am I alive? where does the cause end? where do I begin? do I begin somewhere? Spaniards Creoles Europeans provincials Indians mulattoes patriots royalists who's who? why, the divisiveness of Buenos Aires has no place here on the battlefield nobody knows who the enemy is, neighbor friend buddy relative they mix together for awhile they confront the other I sense my only enemy is the government that sent me to spy on things I don't spy on because I don't remember to do it I only remember to live, if I didn't I'd be dead there's no need to spy on reality already*

*there is no government there aren't any royalists there's
nothing.*

I disappeared from the camp for almost a month, in spite
of the fact that every day a carriage boy would come with an
order for me to present myself immediately. And it was no
happenstance that I could disobey the all-powerful one with
impunity. He knew what I knew. And the terrible secret sealed
off all possibility of penitence.

I asked María to take over my duties, which already took
care of themselves, and, overcome with the fatigue of
hopelessness, I decided to stay in Tucumán to wait for the
tempest. She was the only one I told, although, as always,
she already knew. Wearing nothing more than her skin as I
first loved her, she made haste to console me. After allowing
me to possess her until I discharged all my disconsolation
between her legs, she sat on my bed, which was also hers, lit
a cigar with the candle that I had on my nightstand, and,
scratching my back in just the right spot, laughed at me:

"What did you expect, Tucuman? You should know that
the roads he walks are jest his alone," she said while she
caressed my aching heart.

From that moment on, I stopped being interested in the
fate of the Revolution, regardless that all around me the city
bubbled with preparations and victory.

My sole concern was that Bernardo should not learn of
the treachery that surrounded him. I was not going to tolerate
his knowing that the treasure he guarded more than his life
already had a master; that an errant blue glance had stripped
him of his only purpose.

By then a second Triumvirate, more sinister and despotic
than the first, was already in power in Buenos Aires.

Not only did they not castigate Belgrano's disobedience
but, impressed by the victory in Tucumán, sent reinforcements incredibly quickly. It is so easy to ally yourself with
the victor. Black and Browns, Patricians, and a big shipment

of arms and ammunitions arrived one morning wrapped in a compact dust cloud of promises.

I capitalized on the opportunity. My presence was not indispensable, as I had left everything in order for that extravagance of armaments. It was no longer a place for me.

Days before I left for Salta, I presented myself at his house.

"General, the days of punishment for you and me have come to an end. I free you of my presence. If I continue here with you, there is no doubt that some morning you will turn up dead," I said, obliging him by my gaze not to lower his.

Nothing more needed to be said, but he lowered his eyes and kept the dignity of silence.

"Very well, Rivas, I thank you for your discretion. I did not wish to harm your brother, I swear to you. She will explain it to him soon. She promised me."

"He is not the only injured party," it occurred to me to say, already close to the door.

Dolores carried out her part, and in a meeting full of gasps, distressed lace, and tears, she let an enamored and unsuspecting Bernardo know of her intentions to break their engagement.

The news brought about all the embellishments of a scandal in the Helguera family that already considered Bernardo and his fortune to be theirs. The news spread quickly by word of mouth in Tucumán, as avid for gossip as it was fed up with war. The new romance was so easily taken apart and pieced together again that it was clear that the last to know who Dolores's new master was happened to be my brother and me. That was a solace to our stepmother and her lardy daughters, who always wished us grief.

Bernardo fell into bed, split in two by that rupture, which he failed to comprehend—until he learned who his rival was. And then his descent was deeper still.

Dolores had the firmness of obstinacy and, dazzled at having gained the attentions of the most desired bachelor in the city, she felt triumphant after a battle in which my brother never had the chance to prove himself. There was no pity for Bernardo. He cried, pleaded, threatened, and slept, lying like a dog at the door of her house simply to see her leave and to cling to the hem of her dress. But it was useless. Nothing succeeded in modifying her resolve. The little girl locked herself in her bedroom and did not open her mouth even to eat, having previously announced to her family that she would let herself die if they were opposed to her love. As the days passed, and as her family was won over by her stubbornness, she succeeded in getting permission for the general, as old as her father, to come to call.

The night before the army departed for Salta, María and I cried in each other's arms all night long, aware that our time had ended. Nothing would be the same again for either of us. Life was responsible for leaving us orphaned once again. We had gotten a whiff of our shipwrecked state and our skin caught fire as soon as we touched. Together we knew the delirium of waking up damp, our sweat mixed together and the desperation to repeat our surrender once and a hundred times more. I know, always knew, that I did not possess her completely, that I had of her only what she wished to give me. But it was not a little. Nor did I give myself completely, but it was sufficient to live the most intense moments that my animal self would ever permit. The parts each of us denied to the other had the same master.

Now, all that had come to an end. My moments of happiness were short. But at least I had vanquished the ignorance of love, which had distressed me for forty years.

I stayed in Tucumán. I could not go on up to Salta, leaving behind a brother destroyed by a love gone bad, at the mercy of those three hostile Rivas women who enjoyed our suffering and who, mouths full of crumbs at tea time, spewed gossip.

To keep from thinking, I went back to the field rows, spoke to the foremen, took account of the skinny herds of skinny mules, and rescued from the mold my first scribbles, in which I recognized with tenderness the hasty boy I had also been. And I returned to insomniac nights of writing.

The 24th of February in the year 1813 brought good news to Tucumán. Pío Tristán had been crushed at Salta. No one could now dispute our rights to our own land.

Belgrano was not the only victor. It was the people who, in spite of not knowing very clearly who the enemy was, did not forsake our troops.

They say that the battle took place in the streets of the city in the final moments. Men, women, and children joined in with the army to add hundreds of additional soldiers.

The city of Tucumán let its bells take flight. The festivities and masses of thanksgiving for the victory at Salta took place with a euphoria that for a short time gave them back their lost happiness.

But that success was greater than the general's pride could assimilate, and he became inebriated with glory. Those who returned alive told me about it. Adulations, vivas, conspiracies. Anxiety of greatness, intrigues, and the avid desire for more laurels made it so that one fine day Manuel Belgrano got up and under the power of some Ajogún of María's, commanded: "Army of victors, follow me."

And at an all-out gallop, with no plans, food, or ammunition, he went out to meet the enemy, followed by a barefoot, fanatic group that knew not how to bring prudence to bear, blindly believing in him. His winter headquarters already set up in Potosí, he began to lose contact with reality, mad with omnipotence.

In the last months of 1813, the news began to arrive in Tucumán like curses and people gathered in the streets to cry. The day the first post came announcing the disaster at Vilcapugio, shops did not open their doors, and men and women clamored to know the fate of their sons, brothers, and relatives who, so drunk with victory, had departed as though bound to Belgrano.

Vilcapugio, then Ayohuma. Spilled blood falls like a cataract from the North, drowning Salta, Jujuy, Tucumán. Death oozes from Upper Peru *if your God had to punish you damnation why did He do it when you were with all the boys to top it off they didn't kill you a bunch of young, black Shangós died, scrappers who didn't deserve it you didn't leave any foolish thing undone and nobody not even Lamadrid who is such a scoundrel could stir themselves to tell you to stop screwing around with Masses and to fight once and for all don't look at me to ask for forgiveness I don't forgive you members of government are going to get you they say you will be relieved of command wish to God they'd shoot you hang you what do I have to suffer so much for at this point in my life I'm coming to love this troublesome nation that seems to be dying then in a bit stands up again.*

Belgrano went too far in trusting in God, the Virgin, and his own strength. After the battles of Salta and Tucumán he considered himself to be heaven-sent. He tried to be Alexander, Napoleon, Julius Caesar, and he was nothing more than the executioner of his own men. He penetrated into hostile territory without weapons or food, and with half of his men barefoot and worn-out.

The city of Tucumán wept. I felt responsible, faced by the parents of so many boys I had seen come into this world, boys I had spirited on to defend liberty. How to look again into the eyes of those mothers who, even today, look down when they pass me by.

I withstood the wait no longer and went up to Salta to meet the Army, exchanging spent horses with frothy muzzles at each one of the stagecoach stops, through the thirty-nine leagues that I reckoned were symbolic of eternity.

Just the thought that I would not see María again made me crazy. I imagined her dead, a prisoner, wounded. I felt her to be lost, and I felt the same. And the road did not ever end.

The city of Salta was also in mourning. It had bid the

troops farewell, full of euphoria and so confident in the victory that many women had kissed their men with a casual goodbye, certain they would see them again. Their sobs were louder than the death knell of the bells of the cathedral and the Convent of the Merced. And they were all kinsmen in the face of death's mystery. Grief glided over that city, predestined by its geography to serve as a theater of tragedies. Masses were said, filling the churches with mothers, wives, and sisters who prayed not to be the ones elected by pain.

I couldn't tolerate the city's disconsolation, and hearing the worsening news that came from the North, I decided to continue upward to Jujuy, in anticipation of meeting up with the defeated.

The stupor also arrived in Buenos Aires. They took the victory for granted, even though Güemes announced to the government that only guerrilla fighters, by means of rapid attacks, slit throats, and hearts run through could succeed in this terrain. Belgrano deprived the North of a figure who could have changed history if he had been in Salta. Some time back, in a fit of hypocritical, saintly fury, he'd had Güemes deported to Buenos Aires on account of the passionate love affair he was having with a woman as ardent as he. Belgrano denounced him as a "bad example," and in Buenos Aires, the poor lad got sick from exile, impotence, and prohibited love.

I caught up with them in Jujuy, close to the Christmas of 1813, the worst one of my life. Those soldiers who filed by in front of my eyes were vestiges of human beings. Nothing remained of my companions but tattered ghosts, their eyes swimming with fear. Their bodies had remained back there, escorting the unburied bodies of all the others.

Not even when I hugged her close in my arms was I certain that she was María, my María. I was embracing a specter that was returning from the land of the dead. She had no warmth, taste, or solidity. She did not return my embrace. Her hands, that had closed the eyes of so many dying men, hung lifeless at the bottom of the pockets of her skirt. When she recounted the mistakes her Sir Genrul had made, that she justified as his bad luck, my fury grew:

"He was born with his star blacked out, Tucuman. Luck will never be on his side," she murmured without understanding why I had put a plate of soup in front of her and a spoon in her hand. She had forgotten what eating was, or maybe, in a final gesture of loyalty to her boys, she did not want to nourish herself so as to not feel alive.

I became acquainted with General San Martín in January of the following year. He and his men reached us five leagues from the Juramento River. He had come to relieve Belgrano of command of the few men still alive. In a brief, compassionate ceremony, with horror marking his face, he took charge of the dregs Belgrano was bequeathing him.

The city of Salta, up on its feet already, its eyes dry from weeping, received the names of its dead. On its own, the city had begun to prepare its defenses, given its lack of protection in the wake of the defeats. This time the road was indeed open so the enemy could drop down from Upper Peru, reeling with glory, passing through towns that looked at them dry-eyed as they passed by. They had been abandoned with no officials or weapons. But the enemy did not take into account that the Salteños would not yield.

Repeating the flight of its neighboring Jujeños, the entire city migrated to Guachipas and, in a final show of honor, they wrapped the bell's clappers with black cloth, and with fierce dignity loaded them on the backs of mules, to take them along so there would be no sounding of bells to celebrate the arrival of the enemy. Pushing the children, cattle, furniture, and illusions in front of them, they left the city deserted. Behind their doors, the few who could take up a gun and open fire against the invaders remained behind. Though their future had been made into a wasteland, what sustained them was the hopeful return of their beloved Güemes, for whom they would give more than their lives.

Fury came down from Buenos Aires and landed on Belgrano. He was commanded to return under arrest. Without an escort and vomiting blood, he begins his return in solitude. There are no tears in anyone's eyes. An unjustifiable defeat dries up pity.

With fidelity on her shoulders, María left with him.

I pleaded, begged, and cried so she would stay, like Bernardo with Dolores, and I got the same result.

One cloudless dawn, I saw them draw away, leaving behind a small monument of dust and defeat.

At last, Maria Kumbá!

At last, her moment was heralded that luminous September of 1810. The time had come to delineate with her eyes and not simply with her heart the contours of her longtime companion's face. Many were the years whose grasp held her back, keeping her from running to meet him.

But the time her journey took to get to that September wasn't squandered. Slowly, inexorably, she saturated herself in knowledge and certainty for those uncertain, unknown hours she would spend helping her Sir Genrul, sick from melancholy.

And her eyes became tinged with softness and her hands were dyed with wisdom. And beside her haughtiness, a streak of tenderness grew, and in the shadow of her ferocity, there arose in her the infinite, inextinguishable maternal spirit that she lavished on her boys. It's just that on a par with the warrior, the mother she was called to be was awakening: Mother of the country, Auntie María, the Lady Captain.

When she presented herself before her Sir Genrul, on the eve of the departure for Paraguay, she gave no importance to the unbridled throbbing in her veins. She was too busy making herself into the gaze that would penetrate his soul and live in his heart. Their eyes were freed of their will and they met halfway. Happily, they were introduced to each other, examined each other, became fused together, concave and convex.

And those skittish provinces of the North were the setting where she would grow to take on a semblance of mythological proportions. The battles that would unfold there molded themselves to the rough terrain of an inclement soil.

The 20th of February, the city of Salta awoke, damp from the mist of hostile clouds that covered the hills. He couldn't get up from his cot. He fell straight back, after trying to sit up. The familiar, feared taste of iron flooded his mouth, announcing a geyser of blood that wouldn't delay in convulsing him. Before María Kumbá's eyes, her Manuel attempted to control his illness by the sheer imposition of his desire alone. She turned her eyes away. She couldn't overcome the unending pain of seeing the permanent struggle between his anxiety and his physical weakness. Her imperious, pleading invocations to Shangó so that Sir Genrul could recover part of his waning health had been in vain. The categorical message from her Orishá arrived: A soul so large it couldn't even be housed in a vigorous body; such a case would upset the equilibrium that ought to have dominion over spirit and matter. Only sickness would stop such momentum.

That morning he got up shaky and, disdaining the stretcher, stood before his troops, ready to lead them into battle. Men and animals tried to free themselves from the muddy grip of the ground that clung to their limbs. The victory at Tucumán still remained in their spirits; enthusiasm clarified their gaze and wiped away their frowns, in anticipation of victory over the invader.

Through ravines in the hills the royal troops descended, tracing streamers of death in the air with the weapons in their arms. Rifles in their hands and death in their eyes, a wild mosaic of American battalions awaits them below. Savageness arises from inside them; they spiritedly inhale the air smelling of powder, and slowly but surely begin to bend the will of the enemy who will fall in this distant, foreign land that accepted no owners save those who were born here. And the settled nature of the Spaniards' ideas of subjugation will be paid for by their uprooting at the hour of death. For not one of them will ever know where that man they missed so much had fallen, nor what words he uttered when he died at the hands of Americans.

One has to abandon guiding them toward unhappiness; one has to give up hurting them. (One of the moral commandments of the Odú)

I'm getting tired of sitting. This willow hammock may be comfy, but my bones can't tolerate a long time quiet in the same place. You, sir, will soon get to be old, and then you'll agree I'm right. What a pity you being so silent and not telling me anything. Did you notice that I jest spent the time squawking all by myself? And I 'spose that if you don't go it's prob'ly on account of I'm not boring you.

I was telling you a while ago that tonight the stars make me recall the North. What beautiful places!

Even the air is different than here. Yes, the people are different too, quieter, like you. As though they's passing the time thinking, if they talk at all.

I met a lady there, Colonel Padilla's wife. Look here, I've seen any old thing in my life, but a woman like that one I never will run across again. The time to return to Buenos Aires coming nigh, I found out they named her Lieutenant Colonel. Juana Azurduy was her name. I remember her clear as a bell, nice-looking. Tall, black hair. She could easily stare you down.

She fought better than many a little officer I knew, and on top of that they put on airs of valor. She was born in that country. I met her on Christmas night, don't ask me what year 'cause I don't remember, but it was before Ayohuma. I was mixing up the corn pone that my Sir Genrul took to so much, thinking about the happy face he's going to put on when he saw his favorite dish. He came up to me all serious and introduced me to that lady, so pretty to look at, who was a warrior. I remember it clear. She fought on horseback, beside her husband. No frills about Doña Juana. She made herself loved by everybody. How was I not going to love her when you could spot her courage from a ways off, and her suffering. The poor thing, her four little children died, almost

138

as little as my Agustín, whilst she was hiding from the Spanish for months deep in the mountains without a thing to eat or drink. See if this here Revolution didn't make her suffer, and with her never complaining, keeping up the fighting till she was old.

Well, truth is that I can't complain either. Of what? Why, it was in the army where I felt important for real. And not only for my Sir Genrul, but for all my boys. My little son still alive, he would've been as old as them. I saw my Agustín in them, and I prayed to Yemoja that wherever he was that he had close by a Tía María to be with him. And it would be unfair to complain, because the truth is, in spite of the troubles we went through, of the hunger and the cold we suffered all the time, each chance we had to celebrate something, the ruckus would last till sunrise. In Tucumán and in Salta we put on a big bash right after the battle. I believe that not only was we happy to win, but to be living too. And to feel alive was stronger than the grief for the ones who'd died. Don't take me for twisted, young man, but whoever fought even once knows that's the way it is. Whoever says he didn't feel relief for not being dead is slacking on the truth.

Well, I was telling about the festivities. Those nights there were guitars that played bagualas or vidalas, the gauchos were good at that. Then us blacks and mulattoes would start in. Then and there everybody came over to the smoke to see us dance, clapping their hands along with the drums. We never lacked for somebody to have some sticks or a tumbá drum hidden away in the battalion's gear. Me, on account of jest in case, I always carried around my marapós, and was the one who almost always started off with the music. All the Black and Browns forgot about hunger and their funeral faces went away. Right then and there our desires came out all by themselves and we made a party in between the campfires. We sang and we danced and it was like being again at the feast of San Juan in Buenos Aires. The music was so contagious that after jest a bit, we was all mixed up together, dancing, sweaty and happy. Tucuman Rivas was a caution. He'd start out dancing like he knew how and ended up taking his shirt off, with his trousers rolled up to his knees, his sweat making him shine, and he was one more of us. What a sweet man! Well, at least I took advantage of him good. I satisfied my desires, and he... I'm not even going to say.

I already knew that Sir Genrul didn't much care for the ruckus we made. I never fooled myself, young man. I may have loved him a lot, but I always knew that he couldn't stand us blacks. He had an eye for me, but I knew he said that black and mulatto soldiers were noisy cowards. What do you want me to say? Truth is there's all kinds, jest like there's every kind with whites: cowards who deserted all the time saying that not even out of they minds would they die for whites who didn't want to give them their freedom. And there was also brave souls like Inocencio Pesoa, my buddy, who died on the field of battle. Or like Cock Hat... You didn't know him? He was that freedman who laughed at everything. Antonio was his name, like his master. I met him in Buenos Aires around the time we was fighting against the English. He spent nights waiting for them on street corners, for when they came out of their lodgings good and drunk. They passed by and he popped up behind them to slit their throats, a butcher's good, clean, fussy little slash. We invented the nickname of Cock Hat for him on account of the cocked hat he wore. He didn't ever take it off, even to sleep. He also fought at Vilcapugio and Ayohuma, and since he was fussing all around Teresa, so he could impress her, he helped the three of us a lot when the time came to treat so many wounded.

Once I had to handle a beastly thing, I can't say after which battle. The two were such slaughterhouses that I get them confused. Well, that was the time I had to gather my strength from I don't know where and cut the arm off of one of my boys. He barely had it, grabbing it by the bone. He's jest about dying of pain. I had to stitch it up like a rolled roast of beef. The smell of blood nearly made me throw up. But Ifá guided my hand and the poor soul stayed alive.

But how they did trust in my Sir Genrul there at Ayohuma! We got to that place on our hands and knees, the wind and snow blowing sad and fierce like I can't recall at any other time. I was half-crazy because I knew what was awaiting us. Nobody, not even my Sir Genrul, paid me any mind when I told them we should turn back. Even worse, the Tucuman, who used to come after me jest as soon as it was dark, had stayed in his city taking care of his brother, who kept on lying in his bed, like a dead man, given what happened.

When we came to the flat part, do you know what Goldilocks dreamed up? You won't believe me: he puts us in columns and has the priest say a mass, I swear to you. He missed out on help from his God by praying so much. Not even Orunmila, the powerful, could lend us a hand. Us going at it with the prayers, and the Barbarians quietly settling themselves into the hills that surrounded us. From there they came down and for hours and hours shot off their cannons at us without stopping. Imagine how we fell. A whole passel of Indians fought with us, Cumbay, that part-king, and his men. The majority had sticks and pikes, others only arrows... The poor souls fell like flies. With all the weapons the enemy had, what could they do? Right then and there we sure did lose almost everything, 'cept the flag that Sir Genrul carried close to his side without letting go of it. The few of us who stayed alive approached him like wet chickens and that's how we began to flee from the Barbarians, who were dying with laughter and chased us until nightfall. Don't make me talk any more, will you? I jest told you it does me ill to remember those things, and you playing deaf...

ELEVEN

The memory of her lodged in one side of my heart

I never thought I would miss her so much that even my skin would hurt. The moment came when I feared ending up like Bernardo. I thought I recognized her in every black woman I saw on the street, and like a fool I would approach, just to smell her. I missed her laugh, her understanding, her taste, and much time passed before I could approach a circle of men drinking maté without sorrow threatening to drown me. It also took a great effort to get up in the morning and not find the object of my hatred within reach. The stupid little Goldilocks was not around to blame for everything bad in the world. I discovered that in all those years he had been the best place to deposit my failures.

But the body becomes accustomed to everything, and slowly the memory of her lodged in one side of my heart, and I preserved my sanity. In the period when I decided to begin to live in Tucumán for good was when I was going miss her. As with my books, I turned the page on that most intense chapter of my life, and finished it.

I finally fulfilled my dream of dedicating myself to writing. I wrote without stopping, as if my life depended on it, until I was completely done in. I began to recount fictions that I mixed up with realities. I spawned characters who suffered, loved, and felt as I myself was finally doing. I put words in their mouths that I would have never dared to speak. I made them feel the torments that, before María, I never allowed myself to feel.

I encountered in my writing a refuge so pleasing that for moments I feared that the fiction would entrap me again. But it was enough to look at Bernardo to dispel the fear. I could not allow myself to leave him to his own devices. He had not risen above Dolores's jilting him, which aroused smiles of compassion now that it had public status.

When I found out that María lived in dire straits in Buenos Aires and was barely getting by selling her alfajores, I begged her to come up to Tucumán to end my loneliness. She replied with messages loaded with humor: "My Orishás won't let me move. My skirt is tied down to the floor." But what she did not tell me was that she had no thought of leaving that port city where she obstinately went every morning in her black woolen shawl to look at the horizon, and that her Sir Genrul should be returned to her from Europe. He had that rare virtue, or that terrible destiny, of being able to travel from the heights to the depths, and to go back over the same path again effortlessly. I did not envy him. Those ruptures never scar over.

It took great effort to become accustomed to my province's slower pace after the whirlwind of Lima's bright lights, Buenos Aires's intrigues, and flirting with death during my peculiar stint in the army. But fortunately I had little time to think about myself. Bernardo, my writing, and the demands of our ever-less-prosperous business, used up all my energy.

Attempting to shield my brother from his own thoughts, I opened a shop on the plaza for him to take care of. He moved about resignedly among the customers and spent time with friends. I know he did it to conform to my wishes, but I was not fooled as it was only his body that moved around the merchandise.

I did not want him to feel like a simple shopkeeper. I had bought a prominent storefront that took up the entire north corner and, in belated reparation, I baptized it "Rivas and Sons Department Store."

I had mortgaged the cane fields of Trancas and in a Faustian display offensive to the poverty then rampant, I fabricated a world of a 1001 nights for Bernardo.

You could purchase Castilian dry goods of any sort there. Women swarmed like flies to honey before the array of silks, brocades, Chantilly lace, silk fabric, Cochabamba linen, cambric, silk petticoats, strips of lace, silk stockings, and other resources they used to escape from spinsterhood.

On the other side, separated by a wall of barrels of the best anise liquor and wines, were piles of more prosaic articles for daily use, with reasonable prices that helped me keep the doors open. Chocolates, tanned leather, plugs of tobacco, earthenware chamberpots, bushels of wheat, rice, sugar, corn, and everything one might need for a house could be found there at the lowest prices in the city.

The business served multiple purposes from my point of view. On the one hand, I dreamed that one day a marrying kind of girl who could manage to awaken Bernardo from his stupor would come in to buy yard goods. But it was also a place where Americans and well-established Spaniards met to share a glass of wine and their comments and plans passed from mouth to mouth while they leaned on the counters, which helped to solidify the network of spies that we set up to protect ourselves. Our losses had left us as vulnerable to our enemy as we were puzzled about who he was in reality: the ones from the North or from the South. And together with a handful of neighbors we decided to leave theory behind and form a brotherhood dedicated to the tasks of spying and the management of informants and bribes in order to safeguard our interests. If we didn't do it, we would be unprepared when the time came.

After three years of living in Tucumán, believing that my life was nestled in between wine, books, and neighborhood conspiracies, I saw María once more. It was around 1816, when she returned right on Belgrano's heels. As soon as I embraced her, I covered her with kisses and reproaches. What could he give her that was more important than my love! But despite her poverty and her poorly-healed wounds, she sold alfajores in the Port while doggedly waiting for him to come back. And my body was also doggedly awaiting her in order to inaugurate anew our urgent needs.

The two years spent in Europe were evident in Belgrano's clothes, and the way he looked down on our people.

I confess that the meeting was more of a blow than I had imagined. I thought the passage of time weakened the passions. Dressed to the T's and pedantic, he appeared in that poverty-stricken Tucumán in a dark velvet suit, batiste linen shirt with shirred Flemish lace, Philippine silk stockings, and polished cordovan shoes with double soles. Nothing in him was reminiscent of that sick man in a mended uniform who years before had been stripped of the command of an army for ineptitude. His arrival upset me beyond the personal. I had an intuition that he was contradictory and untrustworthy *now that you came back from Europe you look down your nose at all of us what did you come back so close to me for why do they insist on making you a military man if you failed so many times why don't they let you have an embassy if that's what you like now you even use perfume but you stink with the smell of monarchy I think you're crazy because you talk about the Dynasty of the Inca I don't know what right you have to talk so much if while you were in salons in England here we were getting poorer day by day but to you it doesn't matter if us Barbarians from the North don't deserve another fate.*

Dolores came to life and stopped being the betrothed of an illustrious absence occupied with important European missions in order to be the fiancée of that pretentious character who in no way resembled the austere military man of years past. She stopped writing him those long letters full of love that I would swear he never even opened. And both of them began to display themselves in daily outings in his two-wheeled English fly.

When my brother found out about his arrival, he got up from the bed he almost never left, and with resolute steps he barred the doors of his house and his shame with bolts.

Belgrano commenced to make official visits to the Helguera household, where they had already forgotten Bernardo and his love, and were definitively dazzled by her illustrious catch.

I found María more beautiful than ever. In all those years she had not ceased to inhabit my dreams. We burned in furies postponed by her exile that had left me hungry for her skin and her scent. And I gave myself to become completely satiated with so much oblivion. Luckily, it was the same with her. I was never a foreigner in her chocolate-colored territory. And there were whole days when behind the closed doors of my bedroom, the world turned to ash: "You never give up, Tucuman. That's why I love you so much."

And I happily went back to showing her how much I had needed her.

The city of Tucumán burned with hope. The Congress that would finally declare the independence we needed was in session there. We believed that with it we could put an end to the battles that multiplied incessantly and gorged the phantom of the civil war with the cadavers of brothers.

Meanwhile Santa Fe, tired of Buenos Aires running roughshod over them, had declared itself an autonomous province, and almost all of the North applauded their valor.

"This America is too barbarous for everyone to enjoy freedom," intoned the Porteños, among whom Belgrano was to be counted.

Governments have a very short memory and the people have a long time to pay for their oversights. Forgetting Manuel Belgrano's inefficiency, one bad day they ordered him to take charge of the army once again. In the midst of the applause of his friends, he arrives in Trancas to take command, and to set up his camp in Ciudadela again. No one knew that those troops would not fight the invader, but their brothers instead.

And the tragedy was set in motion that my friend Saavedra had announced years ago. Uprisings in the provinces continued with increasing frequency. To our surprise it was Santiago del Estero's turn. To think that we always made fun of that city on account of the apathy of its citizens and its landscape wrapped in eternal siestas. They taught us a lesson. In a display of wild-eyed bravery, they shouted to the four winds that they were not going to pay any more tribute to Buenos Aires, and even less would they bow and scrape before them as if they were their bosses. Furthermore, they threatened to join Güemes and Artigas, their true equals.

Their attitude was suicidal and ours cowardly, because we ignored the power the united provinces might have had. Instead of that, we looked on with indifference or resignation—what is the difference—as Buenos Aires squashed them.

The Porteño army made its headquarters in Tucumán and, owing to the heat and the palm trees, they slowly lost the order and organization it had cost them so much to impose. Detached, I watched it all from my house and my writing.

Bored with a lack of challenge, the men stopped feeling like soldiers. There was as little enthusiasm as money, and their immobility was so senseless that, in order to alleviate the ennui, they gave themselves with perseverance to maintaining intense amorous relations with those Tucumán women who, as productive as the rich soil, gave birth to hundreds of bastards.

But soon they began to notice that new currents obliged them to line up with one of two bands that identified themselves very clearly, either provincials or Porteños. The waters had been mercilessly divided.

"What kind of mission are we carrying out immobilized here while Güemes and his gauchos are getting killed in Salta?" they asked themselves. And no one gave them an answer.

Tucumán was in a curious situation with the Porteños in the South, and to the North the gauchos who, cut off from all help, stopped the advance of the Spaniards as they could. So much inactivity on the part of Belgrano, who was said to be obeying government orders, began to look suspicious. On every corner irate groups began to rise up over the lack of solidarity with Salta and its needs. And the people's fury turned into insults and harassment when, in 1817, Salta was invaded by the enemy without Belgrano having so much as made a move from Tucumán.

The pressure the furious Tucumanos brought to bear was so great that he had to secretly order my namesake Lamadrid to support the Salteños in that unequal fight, so as to not ignite the ire of Buenos Aires.

Without begging for reinforcements, Güemes only clamored for gunpowder. Without it, resistance was impossible.

Already impatient at seeing that no one was giving concrete answers to the much castigated city of Salta, a group of friends and I traveled to our estate in Trancas and, with sulfur, saltpeter, and carbon that we obtained with some difficulty, we dedicated ourselves to making that item indispensable to Güemes. With our rudimentary knowledge of chemistry, we became a menace to the entire area. But once the powder was prepared, the real odyssey began: we had to get it to its destination by smuggling it past the Barbarians' checkpoints.

Alcohol was their downfall. Making ourselves out to be drovers, we loaded small droves of mules with barrels of gunpowder, except for a few that were filled with alcohol, and it was our safe conduct pass to get to Infernales.

That system, with which we also managed to transport quinine, ammunition, and weapons, lasted several months, until the enemy's high command ordered an investigation into why the men sent to oversee the traffic of wagons at the Posta del Pescado stage coach stop had not been submitting status reports. It was very simple. Thanks to the alcohol there was not a one of them who was fit to pick up a pen, much less of conceiving and composing an idea.

Salta suffered nearly seven years of punishment for being the northern frontier of a government that feigned ignorance of its plight, and Salta had to pay with blood for its location in a territory that was still ill-defined. The entire city was a campground. All the women, old folks, and children were spies, guerrillas, soldiers, and the Spanish could do nothing against a whole populace ready for war.

Their need for weapons was so great that, at the end of battles and with the aid of shadows, people went back to the site and, crossing themselves, took rifles from the cadavers, pledging to have a mass said and to make good use of the weapons.

Unseen in the treetops, children hurled rocks down through the thickness of leaves at the patrols of Spanish soldiers that came out to look for food. And the shower of rocks was so fierce that the children were feared as much as the gauchos themselves.

Skirmishes took place in the streets. So it was common for milkmen, who passed by at dawn delivering their merchandise, to fearlessly step over the body of some Spaniard who had dared to cross the deserted areas at night.

Clouds of the passions that pulled the country this way and that also came to the North, finally unleashing the much-feared wave of violence. The territory was divided in two. Buenos Aires against the hinterland, the rich against the poor.

From 1810 on, this confrontation could be seen coming on. It was known that the day the provinces stood up on their feet, Buenos Aires would punish us mercilessly. And that is how it was. Santa Fe, Entre Ríos, Corrientes, made an illusory proclamation of a utopian autonomy. It lasted a very short time.

Belgrano continued to be artificially paralyzed in Tucumán, little by little losing the respect he had gained years before. It took more and more effort to exhort the troops. He could not go too far since his own private life was an obstacle. His romance with Dolores was all the more out in the open. But in displays of hypocrisy, when he discovered one of the officers or one of the troops drunk from alcohol and lovemaking, he subjected him to severe sanctions, until he passed in front of a mirror and looked himself in the eye. He immediately lifted the punishment of the surprised sinner, who was still under the inebriating influence of liquor or love. His furious fits grew more and more frequent. Bit by bit the hatred for his dark fate, that had promised to be so brilliant, built up and distanced him from those men who would have given their lives for him years before.

During that period, his relationship with Dolores was splendorous. They drove around in his carriage and entered the cathedral arm in arm, without realizing that Bernardo, always himself, cried like an orphan while hiding behind the columns.

And all of it could have gone on like that, suspiciously frozen in time, if it were not for the eternal rolling on of life that tore the calm to shreds.

In the end, death foretold arrived

Off there goes María Kumbá, certain and uncertain, mother and distressed friend. Her gaze can't reach far enough to warm the high plains that foretell of mourning, inhospitably.

There she goes, in the midst of that disheveled army equipped solely with crazy dreams of freedom. Infirmity and discouragement are their inseparable companions now. Bullets will no longer be the only harbingers of death. It will also come with burning fever, paralyzing cold, and hunger that saps the spirit.

There they go, bound to the destiny of the general who one day, overwhelmed by secret voices, mounted his horse and headed off toward the rugged Upper Peru after an enemy that was ill-disposed to renounce the riches of this land.

María was inundated by the unhappy signals the Orishás whispered to her, and whatever she did to slow down the mystical soldier who galloped on in search of a defeat was useless.

There they go, lashed by the wind through that sad, rocky terrain, advancing night and day, white from snow and fatigue, black with hunger and omens, with an illusory miracle on their shoulders. The sheer cliffs of the mountains appear to trick those flatland men who, sliding down with their belongings, proceed blindly through its treacherous ravines. For very few will there be a return. Almost all of them will remain there, planted in the ground.

You should probably multiply yourself, María, together with your daughters, to help so many boys, feeling yourself a debtor in advance for knowing that life won't be taken from any one of your girls. And in the tense hours that precede the battles, only you can implore your gods to have the pity that will never come.

Before her eyes, the General unleashed his personal battle against so much illness that tried in vain to demolish him. The enemy's gods had insinuated themselves in his soul and from inside they piteously tried to destroy him. Fever, vomiting blood, the sweats, all attacked him in waves, clashing against his iron will not to cede to sickly flesh. And implacably, with only a handful of days in the interim, the appointments with death will be realized. Vilcapugio and Ayohuma will be the names of unfathomable defeats.

Extermination takes possession on the fields of battle. Men and mounts manhandle the life that only clings to the strongest. In an obscene counterpoint, one can discern the ordered columns of Barbarians who, with academic precision, spread destruction among the Americans. In those columns, Indians are mixed in with blacks, and gauchos, and creoles, whose bravery is naively armed with arrows, slingshots, and boleadoras.

And it will be in Upper Peru where the Regiment and the Battalion of the Black and Browns will give their lives to end their slavery, unveiling a ferocity dormant under the weight of servitude.

Blurred by death and cannon smoke, our men continue slowly to fall, astonished at the final encounter. The Americans sell their lives very dear. Yelling "Charge!" they look for the chest of the invader who will tumble from his mount never to rise again. And they'll be centaurs who fight for their soil, and they'll be giants who fight for their country.

How little she will be able to do in those hours of destruction for all her sons, poor Lady Captain, Mother of the Nation. Before her eyes those she saw laughing when they still carried happiness up on their shoulders will continue to fall, beyond her protection. Astride her horse, with a saber that extends her desires and her hand, she will draw pinwheels of death in the air, knocking down those who, believing her to be vulnerable, approach to claim her life.

The booming cannons cease after hours of deadly

roaring. The battlefield is sown with cadavers in an infinite number of postures: looking at the sky, surprised to be dead, looking at the ground, as if sleeping. Even the stones, dyed with so much blood, are soaked with pain.

You could do nothing for her boys, Ifá? You couldn't stop so much prolific death? What good is your useless gift of curing now, if it couldn't detain the life that slowly flows out of so many sons of distant mothers, littered all around, unprotected on the indifferent ground?

Their eyes dry with pain, she and her daughters will search among the fallen bodies, greedy for someone who yet harbors life, staunching wounds, wetting parched lips, and they will persuade life to not give up the matter that claims it. And they will hurriedly run to cradle the dying, who, in their final moments, trembling with cold, call for their mothers.

From their womanly mouths will come, like magic, the words that each one of them needs to hear while he steps over the threshold of life, ancient words that with their sound will entwine mother and son together with an imaginary umbilical cord.

Later, she will go to stand beside her Sir Genrul, now abandoned by the enemy gods, who left happy after having whispered false signals to him. With an incredulous gaze, exhausted, he reviews the desolate spectacle of his men surprised by death, obliging himself to fix it in memory. And he will alleviate his deep pain on seeing his dream of extending the Revolution to these provinces vanish, which reminds him that there still exists a yearning that transcends death, that triumphs over destruction: the yearning for liberty.

But he can tell himself that tomorrow is soon enough; today he's covered with bodies.

**Hunter, friend, do not shoot. Come inside the house, come inside. Hunter, friend, do not shoot. Goodness is returning, goodness is coming my way.
(Orin religious chant)**

I talked so much that, in the end, I didn't tell you about when I was a prisoner up there near Salta. I get dizzy myself from hearing me squawk so much. It must be the habit of having nobody who's going to listen to me. Why we're even going to end up being friends when it commences to get light, in jest a bit.

That was the first and only time those wretches put a hand on me. We were close by a river, Piedras I think it was called, narrow with colors wherever you looked. The wind came up every now and again. I was good and worried, moving all around amongst the wounded. They was poorly fed and had only little drops of water here and there. There was a bunch who burned up with fever and hardly enough quinine. I was so fatigued that I didn't have the strength to prepare some small herb teas: Napa thistle, wormwood, and verbena, that do miracles for the dying.

My Sir Genrul didn't sleep from so much work and was a skinny rag of a thing. I was having them look for some neighbor of good will with a cow so he could have something healthy. But they were skinnier than he was, and didn't have any milk neither.

What's worse, from being on a horse so much, the rheumatism got him something fierce. Why, he wasn't so young anymore to be all the time up on a horse. Each time I accompanied him on a campaign, I'd already prepared an oil I put earth worms in, not many, jest a few. First, I left the bottle in hot dung for nine days and nine nights. I moved it from there to a casserole and cooked it over a slow flame. Rubbings with that are the best there is for rheumatism. They give relief as soon as you begin to massage, and for a time he was in a better humor. But not much. You won't believe it. When he sank down into idiocy, it was better to take off running. If I tried to make him eat something, he became furious and kicked me out, yelling. I pretended to be deaf, and after he'd thrown me out, I came back all quiet, and I'd offer him a bitter maté. I used fatigue to beat him. Why, he wasn't bad, jest a fool at times, but the poor fellow had his good reasons.

One, the biggest one, was his disappointment with Buenos Aires. They was real quick to appoint him, but when the time came to send money, they looked somewheres else, and he stayed more alone than a mushroom. You might say of people at the North that the poorer the more generous, because if not...

I don't know if you know that August is a devilish month for the sick. They become like crazy folks with the wind and, if you don't watch out for them, they end up dying. That's on account of there's so much Ajogún going around loose. That's the month when the most sick people are buried.

Well, we was wrapped up in all of it that August, fighting the demons, when other devils fell upon us, those God-forsaken Barbarians. They moved so fast that we didn't have time to defend ourselves. Don't go believing we didn't fight them. What happened was that in the rush and with so many folks mixed up with ours, we got into such a tangle that I'm not even going to tell you about it. There was children playing in between the cannons, nearly blind old folks who crossed themselves in the midst of saber slashes looking for where to hide, and even snot-nosed youngsters who went around hollering and stoning the Barbarians or gathering bullet shell-casings to fill them up again with powder.

My Sir Genrul put his hands to his head upon seeing such disorder. In the middle of that hullabaloo, without even realizing it or my daughters either, they took about forty of us prisoner. They tied our hands and joined us up in groups of five. In a line, they drove us like mules, tied to their saddles, laughing at us. All during those days, they didn't give us water even, and they didn't let us sit neither. Standing the whole time, falling down with sleep. All the worse, I was with the monthly period and the blood was running down my legs. When they realized my skirt was red, they laughed at me and made fun of me. They said I'd saved myself by jest a hair from getting raped. That if it wasn't for my period, they'd have grabbed me with no disgust at all, no disgust...that's what they gave to me. Finally, one of them took pity and he untied me for a time so I could clean myself up. I cut a few strips from my petticoat, and that's how I managed. But the insult to me was enormous, my friend; me among so many men. It even made me ashamed of being a woman.

None of us prisoners complained. We didn't give them that pleasure, and see here, we traveled for days tied up and starving. As soon as he was able to, Sir Genrul gathered together the Indians, gauchos, and fine folks, who followed us from Jujuy, and all of them jumped on that ill-bred bunch. There was such a mess right-off with the heat and the smoke from hayfields the gauchos set on fire to create confusion that nobody knew who was who.

Hiding behind wagons, trees, or close to the river, my boys didn't let up on their firing, furious at seeing me tied up like a cow.

All we could do, still bound up together, was to fling ourselves to the ground and wait until the shooting stopped, trying to free our hands from the thick cords that were digging into our flesh. When we got up, we weren't prisoners any more. From that episode I only remember the shame of being tied up like an animal and jerked along. Right then and there I could understand what a person feels who isn't free. I was never closer to my granddaddy and grandmama, who had been brought over bound-up.

In Vilcapugio I did suffer a great deal. That battle we lost so stupidly that the fury of it still lingers. We came to that sorry frozen campground, like no other I had seen, in the middle of the afternoon, and we withstood it as we could until night. A body couldn't tolerate that cold. The ones who had the worst time was us blacks, who don't even feel the heat but the cold gets into our bones, above all when you been marching such a long time with your belly empty. We was dying of envy seeing those Indians jumping around naked like goats.

When the sun came out the next day, the enemy was already half a league away. Taking advantage of nighttime, those mangy dogs had taken up the best spots for the attack. But my Sir Genrul didn't get left behind as far as rascally goes, and up on the ridges that ringed the flats, he ordered the two thousand Indians who'd jest joined us to make a line. So, from a distance they put such a fear in you that nobody was going to find out the poor devils was unarmed. It was jest that teensy bit we lacked in order to win. Sir Genrul had already ordered bayonets placed, and my boys advanced on the Barbarians like lions. Right then and there what happened happened. I heard it crystal clear because I'd stayed near the Indians on top of a hill. In the middle of the Spaniards running off like rabbits, you could hear a call for retreat. Yah-sir, do not look at me like I was crazy, it was a bugle sounding retreat. It'll never be known who the sad individual was who blared it out—some enemy god took charge of it—but the bugle was ours, I'm certain of that till this very day.

Right there our luck changed, and my boys, disoriented, turned halfway around and, firing at the hillsides, wound up being chased by the enemy. My Sir Genrul became a crazy man, grabs up the flag and, ordering the drums to follow him still beating, led the boys to the top of a rise. But, what! Not even four hundred survived. By nightfall we began the retreat. We carried the wounded on burros and llamas, in the middle of a darkness that I won't even tell you about. The grief and pain from seeing so many dead all together made us weep.

We suffered such hunger that when day was almost breaking, as we came to some rundown dirt farms, we lit out without a pause to devour some llama meat they made us a gift of. We didn't even notice its foul odor from age, as hungry as we was. That's how it went with Goldilocks. The vomits had so much of a grip on him that that time I believed he was dying on me. With him sick, we couldn't go on, so I did everything I could to make sure he got better as soon as possible. I laid him down in an abandoned shack full of spiders, and some attentive folks around there helped me. I managed to give him baths with Shangó's yuyos for strength and to suck the evil spirits out of his body. He was doing so poorly that he didn't even have a notion that I had him naked, wrapped in a dirty blanket. The whole time he appeared to be asleep. Although Tucuman found no pleasure in it, he ended up assisting me. As I could, I boiled up plantain, nettles, sarsaparilla, and cayenne. I'm never without those yuyos that can cure jest about any old thing. He helped me give him part of a bath, which isn't the same as a real bath.

After three days, the Goldilocks opened his eyes, and we could get on with our fleeing. He never found out that all that time we was bathing him with his butt in the air like a newborn.

Up there, we were starving for real, days and days with nothing to eat. Those that could bestir themselves sucked on the flesh of cactus pears even though they filled their mouths with spines. That was better than being thirsty.

What a thing hunger can be. Once in Potosí they sent us supplies that contained rotten jerked beef and mutton. Do you think it disgusted anybody? Ha! Smell and all, we jest put lemon on it and ate it like it was the tastiest morsel in the world. Don't make that face, my friend, you have to live to know. Anyone hasn't suffered by going without, how can he know about what a body will do to stay alive!

TWELVE

So then I decided to kill him

When Belgrano officially asked for Dolores Helguera's hand, the first symptoms of insanity began to appear in Bernardo. Voices, laughs, and cries emerged from his bedroom. On entering, we found him talking to himself, looking at himself in the mirror, and uttering gibberish.

Seeing my desperation for this brother who had been converted into my youngest child, Inés consoled me and herself.

"It will pass, Chil' Gregorio. The pains of love come as they go. One nail drives out another." But I knew that the nail was so hammered in that no other would take its place. It was already a part of him.

One afternoon when Bernardo's howling was beginning to drive me crazy, I called for María to see if she could help him with a conjuring. She came trying to hide the pain she felt for her Sir Genrul, who would soon have another mistress.

They were closed up in the room for more than an hour when she came out shaking her head.

"So he can entertain himself and perhaps stop suffering for a time, I told him that some Tuesday at 10 at night he should write the name of that woman on a sheet of parchment, that he should then put it under his pillow, and every night repeat some words I dictated to him. He'll be distracted but no more. I'm not going to fool you, Tucuman, Chil' Bernardo exists no more."

At that moment I did not understand what she wanted to tell me, and I did not want to ask her. Grief drowned my comprehension. Bernardo did not deserve the life he was living. What harm had he caused with his blandness? Was

Belgrano not content just making my life impossible? What debt did we Rivas have to pay? Waves of hatred welled up in me.

A month before, by way of a thick wad of money, we had managed for the three fat Rivas women to spend a season at the estate in Trancas so Inés and I could deal with Bernardo more comfortably, without witnesses. One day there were knocks on our door. The person who had come was Jerónimo Helguera, Dolores' older brother, and a long-time intimate friend of Belgrano's.

In a few words he allowed the truth to explode: Dolores was pregnant and Belgrano, the responsible party, was not going to marry her, at least not for now. Her mother was in bed, mortified with shame. Knowing Bernardo's sentiments, she implored him, she begged him to protect her daughter's stained honor with his love. Now they were coming to beg for the pity they had not shown. Why had they not done so when Dolores strolled around happily on the arm of that bastard?

I shoved him out, saying that Bernardo would have the last say.

That very night I presented myself at Belgrano's house. I entered without knocking on the door. María tried to stop me, her eyes full of knowing. As always, he was writing his interminable letters by the light of a lantern. It was easier than having to look someone in the eyes while talking to him.

"Have you lost your senses? Are you so crazy you cannot repair the damage?" I was yelling at him, for the first time treating him as an equal. My power over him had depended on never, under any circumstance, ever raising my voice. It was the weight of my words that set him off. But that time he was my superior.

"I am not going to give any explanations, Rivas. Go away. This is my affair." Then, understanding struck me like a bolt of lightening: Dolores was only an instrument for his final vengeance. He did not have the courage to tell me the truth that was drowning him and poisoning him. He aimed at my brother, the weakest part of my heart.

"You are going to regret this, you little blond piece of dung, I swear to God."

My voice, already calmer, achieved its old effect. He went from white to red. But now it was different. Our faces were already wrinkled and, as is known, the harm we do at such an age is inevitably more damaging than when youth softens the pain.

The very day I told Bernardo the truth, choosing my words to soften the blow, the little reason he had left definitely came unraveled. Like the black butterflies of summer, all the pain hiding under his meekness was released to flutter all around him. The lesions that marred his soul appeared: to have killed our mother at birth, Francisco Rivas' clumsy tutelage, the loneliness his own flesh and blood had left him in, the treachery of his only love. The weariness of it was too much for him.

He cried for seven days and seven nights locked in his room. The Helgueras came and went obsequiously asking after my brother's health, and they prayed he would not die without making the bastard legitimate. They looked on with horror at how Dolores' unmistakable belly grew prosperously.

In the meantime, the whole city gleefully tore her apart: "Sir Genrul's wench, that wretch, how shameless she was."

"And him, every bit a gentleman. There's a reason he's not getting married."

"Surely the child is not his."

"Who knows how many she's been with, the brazen hussy..."

And everyone threw the first stone.

Dolores, also confined to her room, wept with disenchantment over being abandoned. She never understood what had happened to her Sun King, nearly her father, who turned as pale as death when she gave him the news and disappeared with some excuse. She recounted later that they had to punish her until she fainted in order for her to accept marriage with Bernardo. Not because she hated him, but precisely because she believed Bernardo, so dogged in his devotion, did not deserve to be punished on account of a disgraced wife.

When at last he opened the door to his bedroom, Bernardo appeared happy and resolute, completely removed from everything that was not his reality, his vision turning its back on sanity.

"Come, Gregorio, quickly let us ask for Dolores's hand. My father wants the wedding as soon as possible."

The ceremony took place in secret, in the midst of a sadness full of smiles that did not succeed in warming that crisp morning. The only one happy was my brother and that was enough for me. He was belatedly fulfilling the only dream of his life, and the joy he felt was so great that he never realized that nestled deep, very deep in his bride's eyes, was the anguish of abandonment, stronger still than the cord she nourished the child with.

But the inevitable happened. Given the natural condition of life, Dolores' stomach began to be enormous, to move, it took its spot in Bernardo's space, and with one big yank brought him back from the world he had inhabited.

When he faced that truth, so remote and so round, Bernardo lost himself completely. He began to bang his head against the walls and to look for objects with edges to cut himself and bleed till he passed out. His enormous love poisoned him from the inside and made him utterly insane. He panted and went about on his hands and knees, and we could hardly pull him away from Dolores' swollen belly. Each time he looked at it, his attacks overcame him so terribly that he hovered over that full moon, meaning to destroy it. Inés and I were incapable of tranquilizing him, and not even drops of laudanum could calm him.

It is clear that enemy gods allow no repose.

The political bosses in the interior, naively drunk on the previous victory, decide to make known the weight of their horses' hooves by claiming their rights. They defiantly look at Buenos Aires, which for the first time trembles at a threat from the interior.

The undeniable command comes from the government that the Auxiliary Army of Upper Peru should leave the northern border unprotected and march against its brothers.

At that moment, the secret motives for so much silence among the soldier boys in my city came to light. Buenos Aires was saving them for its own protection, without caring about Güemes's immolation.

In the face of my angry astonishment, María left for Santa Fe with her Sir Genrul, on the way to a fratricidal war that made no sense to those of us who had slept for so many years under the stars of the hinterlands. Given all the injustice that María now endorsed with her faithfulness, I began to hate her. I was on the verge of striking her; how could she do that to me? I insulted her, without being able to demonstrate to her the infamy of staying with him. "He makes bastards and is one himself. He is going to kill provincials, stupid, don't you know that? How can you stand by someone who always hated your race, our race? You traitor. No wonder you get along so well."

My capacity for understanding had been drained. I could not accept such servility. I could not, and continue loving her. I decided to remove her forever from my life.

It was then I decided to kill him. A person so dangerously disdainful, a destroyer so cowardly, did not deserve to live. I was not going to allow him to know his son, and even less to learn of my brother's insanity, unleashed because of him. And worst of all was that he would spill the blood of provincials. After so many years of suffering Buenos Aires' pridefulness, he had not learned a thing.

Those nights when María would whisper to me her magic spells and secrets after I made love to her all came back to me with the tidiness of revenge. Also of use was what I had heard in my youth when, hidden behind the tall stoves in the kitchen, I spied on the rituals of the black and mulatto women who invoked the death of some ingrate. And so I began my labors.

Sooner or later his end would come, but in no great span of time. Painful, bitter, just what he deserved. I now had no pity. Hatred is stronger than forgiveness.

And one night at twelve on the dot I began the death spell. The effectiveness of the spell depended on some part of it having belonged to the one being called, which is what conveys the right to make the call.

Not eating or drinking the whole night, I began to whisper his name. My mouth filled up with: Manuel, Manuel, Manuel, Manuel, Manuel... A hundred, a thousand times a night, his vowels and consonants rose up in my throat, filled my mind, and in a deadly throng they ran to meet him wherever he might be, to fulfill their assignment.

They say that a person's strength lies in his name and that from repeating it so much that strength is spent. After so many months of repeating the ritual, when the seventh moon comes, the fatal moon, the unfortunate one realizes he is being called. And tortured by pains, with the ashen color of people with weak hearts, the one called dies.

María told me about it once, without knowing that by revealing her secret to me, she had condemned her beloved Sir Genrul to his death. It was when she put a curse on Dorrego, despite my entreaties not to do it. His had been a tepid, patient curse, so his end took years in coming. But she also told me there were shortcuts to hasten death. And I used them.

When Inés found me calling death, filled with hatred toward that devil who had driven her Chil' Bernardo insane, she was furious with me for not having asked her for help.

"Chil' Gregorio, you won't be able to do it alone. Let's

us go to Mama Gervasia's Sala. The spells she works nobody undoes."

At first I refused. I did not want to share with anyone the pleasure of my final vengeance. But Inés convinced me of the importance of working together.

We got to the Sala on a moonless night when all the Tatas Brujos and Mama Gervasia were gathered there. The news of my revenge had made the rounds among the blacks in the city with the speed of rancor. The majority of them had worked in the "musenga," sugar cane, as they called it, and they lived tranquilly, with dignity from that work. Until they were dragged off from it because of the violence, and rounded up like cattle to be drafted into the army. They were eager to avenge their ancestors by hastening the end, already visible in the distance, of that general who had scorned them as barbarous cowards so many times that not even the storytellers could recall how many.

That place, lit with candles and booming with the frenetic, menacing beat of the bass drums, ignomos, marímbulas, and marapós, gave me goosebumps. The aroma of incense, mingled with others I did not recognize, made me dizzy. I was in the right place. Only a shove separated him from his grave and we were going to give it to him.

We formed a circle surrounding Mama Gervasia. As if by magic a chicken with black feathers appeared, flapping its wings like crazy, its legs tied with a red ribbon. They put it down at the feet of Mama Gervasia, who began to pronounce unintelligible words, already in a trance. As the frenzied beating of the small drums increased, that black woman fell on the floor in the grip of contortions and the cries of those present who gave thanks for the arrival of the god invoked.

When the movement stopped, Mama Gervasia, with a faraway gaze, got up, went over to a little table covered with liturgical objects, took fresh wax and made a human figure.

I could see a lock of Belgrano's blond hair sticking out of that figurine, no doubt obtained by one of the blacks who cleaned his quarters.

In the midst of the unceasing rhythmic chants, she took a small dagger from her bodice and approaching the animal, she sliced its throat clean. The body, separated from its head, continued to move for a few more seconds, splattering all of us with hot, sticky drops of blood. Between her cries, she brought the wax figure close to the spurting blood so it got completely drenched, then raised it up high and began to call the gods of death, who obeyed and came, and she prayed to them in a hoarse voice: "Let him not have peace, tranquility, or quiet. Let unease penetrate to the marrow of his bones. Let him not eat but the food should harm him. Let him not drink but the drink churn his guts. Gods of death, fulfill your obligation." Then she threw the wax figurine into the fire, which gave off a pestilent smoke. She picked it up, now deformed, and put it away in a dark armoire, out of the way of indiscrete glances. Vengeance was served, the gods had listened, and we celebrated until dawn drinking oti, the sacred beverage.

The next day, without yet being able to extinguish her hatred, Inés informed me that she had given a black man who was supposed to reach the general's columns a goodly quantity of yellow bird of paradise, opium poppy, vizcachera macho, and tulisquín flower so that all ground up they could be conveniently added to his meals.

The first days of May 1819, in between screams and loneliness, Dolores, aided by Inés, who refused to carry the newborn in her arms, gave birth to Belgrano's daughter. "Stupid little blondie," I whispered to her. She was identical to her father. And she moved right into my heart.

Bernardo passed through periods of light and shade. He swung between love and hate for Dolores and her daughter. He could not choose one sentiment over the other and that accentuated his insanity.

By the time Belgrano returned to Tucumán in September, my brother had gotten Dolores pregnant in a final act of possession that allowed him to be compensated. And in the end, he chose insanity where he could find a comfortable refuge. Tired of struggling against the lack of love he knew from the time of his birth, he went inside himself where no one would bother him.

Inés and I had it known around that Bernardo Rivas had gone to Bolivia on business for an indeterminate period of time. And one moonless night we sent him to the remote country estate of our friends, the Lugones, in Santiago del Estero, where they had the habit of not asking any questions and making their warmth felt. There among the thistles and the saltpeter flats, the arid condition of the ground is so terrible that, with no onlookers, it was the perfect home for the specter my brother had become. In the absence of anyone or anything that would prompt him with ridiculous demands, he made friends with the animals, the moon and the stars, always well disposed to confidences, and at last he managed to be happy.

We went back to making our Tucumán salons pleasant, where people continued to skin Dolores alive, this time as an abandoned wife.

Manuel dies full of anguish

At last Manuel learned that spiritual defeats kill more completely than other deaths.

And she cried for him, for her divided country, for his foretold death, for the years to come, for the few smiles that luck furnished her. There is nothing to take for consolation.

And that is why his body preferred liberating death. In his final hour he elected rebellion.

To know so soon that the Constitution was a document written to bring about division was the coup de grace.

What more remained to be done than to set out on the easy road toward death?

Life didn't save him any humiliations; it didn't free him from misery. There was no pity for María Kumbá's fair Manuel. There is never any compassion for the chosen.

Anarchy unfolds obscenely before his eyes in those last days, as if it wished that he leave this world asking himself if all the grief had been worth it. María Kumbá cried for him, but he was already far beyond any aid, nor did her gods want to delay the farewell; they said they prefer to hasten it. So much pain, for what...

María ought to have calmed down; the plan was already completed. She closed Manuel's eyes while he was in her arms. He was covered with oblivion in a terrified city that the gods came down to punish that 20th of June, giving it three governors all on the same day.

His last words were for that nation he believed in, but at the moment of his death they were transformed into anguish.

Poor Manuel returned to his voices...

Those who sow the seeds of evil, plant them on the heads of their children.
(One of the 13 Yoruba Rules)

Come, sir, don't be offended. Go on and grab that chair and sit down in front of me. Being old's not contagious. I can see you don't want to tell me who you are, but, friend, why, you spent the night listening to me.

Look, the morning star's already appeared. Right quick the roosters will start to crow. How will this day treat me? I swear to you I'm so worn out that I have no wish for it to begin...

I don't want to even remember how Sir Genrul came back from a trip to Europe. Full of frills, like the little Missis when she went to a ball, I almost didn't recognize him in those strange clothes he was wearing. I'd always seen him in uniform, but what he had on...

He made himself seem so important he didn't want to receive me. Me! He was going to tell me no! I burst in unannounced, and I even pounded on his desk. My goodness, he wasn't going to attend to me, who'd washed the blood off him, the vomit, the sweat. Me, who'd used the eres shells to cure him... Look see if he wasn't going to attend on me. Real shy he was after that scolding. From then on we went back to being friends and he asked me to go with him again to Tucumán. He was saying that he couldn't stir himself to go alone, but I knew it was on account of him expecting a big row with that Dolores person he played dirty, to take away from Tucuman's brother. I suspected from the first what a ruckus was going to be made. Nothing good comes from taking a woman from another man.

And look if it didn't happen. Not even I could stop that Rivas, who went out of his mind when Chil' Dolores showed up pregnant. That sure is no good. I sang it out to him clear as a bell. A child is a gift of the Orishás. You can't go around denying your own blood because that will sure bring a great punishment down. I asked him why did he get involved with making babies if he knew all that it would drag along with it. But he stayed silent. When he wanted to play the fool...

The worst of that little trifle was when Tucuman's brother lost his wits, but really lost them. I went to his house and I put a spell on him to drive out the demons he had inside. I locked myself up in his bedroom and I put river water in a vial, jest a bit, threw in three pinches of ordinary salt, and I prayed to God, the Virgin, and Ifá; all together they're more powerful. The boy began to twist about and fell down in a faint, whilst all the demons was leaving from inside of him. Don't you laugh. Only the ignorant don't believe in the devil. Afterwards, I cleansed the entire place with rosemary, rue, camphor, incense, and cinnamon. When he came to, the demons had already left him, but he stayed like that. Crazy, but like a little lamb. If I hadn't done that, he'd have killed all of them. And if he had killed them all, what do you want me to tell you? It was to find the sense in it. Right? With all the harm they done to him...

I had a solution for everything. I can tell it all to you, sir. All in all, it doesn't suit me anymore. Not a one of my daughters wanted me to pass on to them what Mama Basilia gave to me. They said that they weren't that crazy, that you suffer a lot, and that I was a good example of it.

To calm down the ones who get carried away there's also a solution and it isn't with sticks. I got tired of using it with Goldilocks and Tucuman without they even realizing it. You had to be between them all the time to see them like two fighting cocks. They didn't let any single thing go. If it hadn't been for me more than once they'd have gone to fisticuffs. For certain Tucuman would've won. He was mighty big for being half-Indian, and on top of that he had the power of fury. Jest as soon as I saw them coming, with all their anger on them, I would stand up between and holler: "With two I look at you, with three I tie you up, your blood I drink and your heart I split in two." They took such a fright upon hearing me that their fury ended in a sigh. They knew I was a witch, whatever their doubts... At times fear is no fool.

There's also a secret for calling luck because I don't know if you know it, my boy, but luck has to be called for, or forget it. That's what happened to my Sir Genrul. He paid me no mind and luck got mad and turned its back on him forever. You search for a small lemon, the greenish ones, two garlics, mint, incense, and salt. You dip it in seven basins of holy water, and upon wetting the mixture in each one you say: "Free me from my enemies who wish me ill." If only he'd minded me...

What they didn't know was that those spells weren't from Mama Basilia. They taught them to me at the North. Up there magic goes around free in the hills and anybody can learn it. That's a peril because they use it for good and for evil.

But what I did to do good, and so saved the life of more than one of my boys, was to offer them to Shangó and put them under his protection.

For that they had to wear a ribbon or a red string tied on their wrist till the day of their death. If it got old on them or if it broke, right then and there they had to tie another one on. After the string, I took them to the foot of some tree where they had to leave rum and tobacco for the Orishá. But so's the aid was more powerful, because those were times of war, you had to obtain the blood of some animal to wet the roots, and the mud that it made they had to carry in little pouch around their neck.

In the midst of such poverty, to find a rooster with the best blood, that was more than a miracle. So I'd best not tell you the kinds of critters my boys brought to me because you'll run away disgusted. Shangó too, who understands these things, was in agreement and would take care of them for me during the battles.

Shoot, my arm's beginning to pain me. I didn't tell you about my arm? Uf! Why, after so much fighting nothing of mine stayed healthy, I swear to you. It got mangled on me. Where did it happen? Look, I'm old and I don't even recall...

Well, it happens that that time we were jumping back and forth to push cannons up those ravines with rocks in them that poke into the bottom of your foot. Hurrying as always, taking advantage of the night, with the enemy right on our heels. I was helping by pushing from behind because the slope was something fierce. And when I least expected it, those lazy bums up front let go of the cannon and it comes down toward me. On all fours, I got to one side, but I didn't save myself from being knocked down, and one of the wheels went over my right arm. Truth is, I tolerated it better than a number of men I know...didn't even cry out when the doctor gave my arm a big tug to sit the bone again. But jest the same I stayed out of kilter because one arm ended up shorter than the other, sort of crippled. But how am I going to compare my suffering with poor Doña Juana's who lost her four little sons.

But she wasn't the only brave one I met up there. To see him fight was to see Shangó himself releasing fire from his eyes. He was a crazy man, with that black beard to put the fright in you, killing whoever crossed him. But he was as good as bread, he laughed out loud over anything at all, and his men loved him as though he was their father. I'm speaking of Güemes, that Salteño who died so young, the poor thing, with so much still to do. When I met him he had the color of death close-by. But you saw him looking so healthy, with so much will to live that I thought, "What luck. This time I made a mistake."

Pity be I made no mistake at all. He died a year after my Sir Genrul. I heard tell they killed him like a dog, by treachery. He deserved that less than anybody. His gauchos were left without a leader his equal, and they say that, after that, the battles were never the same again.

Neither did Tucumán go back to being the same for my Sir Genrul when he returned from Santa Fe sick. It was the

November before he died. Restless as that city was, truth is I never cared for it. That disgrace of a city had no better idea than to declare itself independent jest when my Sir Genrul was dying a beggar's death. You won't believe me, but people from his own army wanted to go and put chains on his legs. Why he was stretched out on the bed and couldn't even get up! What a pack of insanity and treachery all together! I never saw my Sir Genrul with so much pain in his eyes, not even the day he died. Luck had it that the English doctor was there, that soul of God, the only decent Englishman I ever knew in my life. He had such a fit of anger when he saw those chains they wanted to put on him that he took the corporal who gave the order by the throat. Nearly killed him.

Luckily, they didn't touch the Goldilocks. But those perverse devils put a sentry at his door because they said he was arrested. What a novelty! It'd been months that the illness had him imprisoned in his bed. What need did they have to humiliate him like that for?

THIRTEEN

No one can survive being forgotten by those who once applauded him

I saw María again when I decided to look for her as impulsively as I had cursed her and pushed her away from me. Of course I tried to forget her, but how do you separate yourself from people who are essential, that one has been close to like clothing.

She went away with Belgrano and returned to Tucumán with him, at the beginning of 1820, when he came back from his latest failure in Santa Fe, and lay prostrate in the bed he would not get up from. Arrangements were quickly made with his family to remove him from that situation and deposit him in Buenos Aires. On his sickbed, he served no cause.

One morning I knocked on the door of his house, taking María by surprise. I did not even want to go in. Our hands clasped together, we tried to communicate to each other the emotion of our final meeting, knowing that only the wounded die of love. For a moment, very old caresses smothered us and we felt that our bones had conquered time. I was even surprised she did not offer me a bitter maté. But it was only that, an instant. Death had already moved in between us and our eyes; hiding the truth, our eyes no longer sought each other out.

"What have you been going around doing, Tucuman? I'm going to know if you made mischief for him."

Of course María would go with him. I had already resigned myself to thinking of her as his shadow. She was leaving my life, definitely this time, at the side of Sir Genrul, with whom death and my revenge had caught up.

I let her go, knowing then that nothing could be done. The causes for her fair Manuel's agony separated us forever. I knew I would run that risk and I took it.

The damage Manuel Belgrano did to my life was tremendous. The battle we joined from our time at the Colegio de San Carlos finally had a victor. And though it might seem the opposite, it was not exactly me.

I saw them set off one early morning in January. It was not the stupid little Goldilocks, but just another ghost among the ghosts of all the dead at Vilcapugio and Ayohuma who escorted him on his final journey. I could hardly make him out among so many specters.

Indifferent to the odor of death, María along with Jerónimo Helguera, Dolores's brother, helped him clamber up into a carriage hired with borrowed money. A strange story, that one, of a brother turned into the shadow of the person who had stained his honor *goodbye forever stupid little Goldilocks we'll never see each other again I don't know if I'm free or lonely you leave me with nowhere to deposit the hate I've carted around since my birth it's going to be an effort to become accustomed to that side of me you're leaving empty I'm never going to tell you about it because I want you to die without knowing it but you left me an inheritance that from now on will be the only thing that will keep me alive and it is this love that I now feel for the nation I inherited from you when I saw you sick or proud solitary or in company a failure or triumphant wrong or right but always obstinately believing with no limitations in a country you already imagined that was worth living or dying for but you will never know about it from me and I won't forgive you either how long it took that first brief touch that flowered in the territory of our only true meeting to arrive.*

The news of his death came in the mail from Buenos Aires, one day at the end of June 1820, when the port city was beginning to lose its power.

I found out like any other citizen of Tucumán that had apathetically allowed him to leave. The spell had done its work. I do not remember if I felt sad, happy, or repentant. When I traveled to Santiago del Estero to tell Bernardo, he was only interested in introducing me to his friends the animals. He remembered absolutely nothing of the past. God had blessed him with forgetting, and now finally he smiled again.

There were not many signs of pain in Tucumán owing to the death of that Sir Genrul who one day had filled the city with glory. No one, no matter what he does, can survive being forgotten by those who once applauded him.

The Helgueras, feigning civic grief, had a mass said for him, which was attended by enough people to fill the first ten rows of pews in the chapel of Nuestra Generala.

Dolores cried, hugging her little daughter, but remained forever in the dark about what had happened to her life. Her pain filled me with guilt. I looked at that baby whose father, as a last wish, had the courage, though not much of that, to recognize her as his own. In his final letter, he asked the only friend he still had to send him news of his "little goddaughter," without daring to write the word daughter.

Poor girl. I felt her in my blood. She existed because I existed.

My sad sister-in-law could not stand so much punishment and after her second child was born, this time my nephew, a real Rivas, she went to live in Catamarca, where no one would ever know of her yesterdays left in rubble.

Of course she quickly got the approval of her family who were fatigued at having to hide themselves away from scandal-mongering, and who wanted their social life to begin again.

I was his godfather, and at my request he became another Francisco Rivas. I hope he has gained strength from the love his grandfather concretely refused to give his own sons.

How distant 1810 and all its conflagration seems to me! That was the start of the period that finally gave meaning to my life. Only those passions justified the passage of time that has delivered me today to the threshold of my end.

I hope I am not judged too harshly. My hatred was

superior to any other feeling. Do not believe that I have been released from Manuel Belgrano. His ghost accompanies me everywhere. It is not a friendly ghost, nor is it hostile. It is a fatally sad, hopelessly anguished ghost. When he approached Bernardo to ask for his forgiveness, my brother started to howl with terror and to drool. And the specter, weeping bitterly, never visited him again.

I am repentant that I invoked his death, not because I did not want to bring about his end, but because with his death mine came too. From the day he died he has been clinging to my shadow. He leaves me not an instant of peace. He sits at my table, he lies down in my bed, he mounts my horse that he keeps in a permanent state of terror. He looks at me all the time, asking me in silence what I did to him, what happened between the two of us, and thanking me for liberating him from life. But my worst punishment is all that he continues not to tell me.

I would have liked to ask him why such meekness in accepting his ill-fated star, why his fatalism in the face of his often contrary fate? But to do so would have meant lowering the shield of hatred. And afterwards? I would not have the strength to withstand so much truth.

It is useless. Even today, when I know that Bernardo no longer suffers, I cannot be at peace. How remote that word always was for me. I never gave it the space to accompany me. I looked for it as much as I looked for my place in life, which I never found either.

When I returned from Lima, it was due to my belief that my place was in Buenos Aires, publishing my American ideas. When I left for Paraguay, I believed my place was in that belated, unnecessary revenge I had invented. When I stayed in Tucumán, I thought that from there, without abandoning my brother or my writing, I could aid the cause more than down there in Buenos Aires. Always seeking and always straying. Even falling in love with the wrong person was the wrong way to live the splendor of love, a punishment for who knows what faults. To this day, I do not recognize them, though just now I can sense them. And although it is barely foreseen, the truth that begins to appear wounds my soul.

I believe, better yet I am certain, that my ultimate redemption came when I made the struggle for the land, for my land, my own. Not for inherited ideals, not by order of Buenos Aires, but rather for the concrete piece of the world that my father left me, for the tangible spaces of dirt we stand upon. And that we continue to stand on.

I suspect that these wars that still have not come to an end will never end. Those who govern Buenos Aires will have children, grandchildren, great-grandchildren, and great-great-grandchildren who will think as they do, that we are their vassals.

And we will have children, grandchildren, great-grandchildren, and great-great-grandchildren who will also think as we do, that they are wrong.

I fear that till the end of the times we live in, we will inevitably continue to be us and them. Them from Buenos Aires, us from the interior. And the war will go on without bullets, but as deadly as it is now.

And if my people will accept my counsel, despite all my confessions and all my sins, please allow me to give it to them. "My" people, the dark-skinned ones from the interior, please know that our dignity was never for sale, that the people from Buenos Aires do not have nor will they ever have the dominion that comes from belonging to these lands that no one could ever enslave. With luck, they will boast of the title of England's most obedient lackeys. And that is not enough. It will never be enough in order to keep standing upright.

Your time has come, Kumbá of the blacks

With prolific joy she went about completing her mission. She could have ignored her inner voices that continued whispering where the path was, but she preferred the challenge of action, and her steps adjusted themselves to it. She returned to the place she'd come from, soft warrior, harsh mother.

Cataract, tumultuous river, inclement rain, vital current. Liquid or solid, she satisfied her calling.

She made life pay for the debt of her mother's and her grandmother's suffering, and they were the warriors she was.

She was punctual at every place she promised to be, and her eyes lit up with gratitude for the Orishás who never abandoned her.

In her final hour she came to understand Ifá and to be reconciled with him, when she comprehended why so much blood was shed that her entreaties had not been able to forestall, so much death that her prayers did not successfully mislead.

And in spite of the pain that pierced her when she cradled her loved ones as they died, she gave thanks that her arms were their final contact with life.

The last time she did that was when she found meaning in her mission. When the sad eyes of Sir Genrul fell on hers, devoting his last glance to her, the reason why exploded in her soul. At that moment, while she attended him in his slow agony, she saw a distinct image in the dying man's gaze, as if it reflected the image of the person he yearned for. Because among so many gifts she received from Shangó that night in June, was the gift of being the measure of his final hour.

Inhabited by a thousand presences, the one the departing soul needed near him blossomed at the moment of his death. And it was his distant mother, the inattentive loved one, the fickle friend that the spirit of every dying man called out for.

And when her general, sick from poverty and oblivion, decided to die, it was that negated presence, that prohibited shade that made him sick of love, marking him forever with the gaze of the impossible. So, when she approached him in a wrenching farewell, his blood took wing and at last sadness fled defeated from his eyes. He departed with his hand in hers, freeing himself forever from his fragile coil, far beyond the puny memory of the masters of forgetting.

When he went, leaving her fatigued by absences, she implored the gods to save her from memories by taking her with them. But Shangó did not listen to her, and she was supposed to continue being the tie that bound the Orishás to their helpless children.

And until her time came she was the steadfast protector of her blood brothers, who sought her out knowing her to be the messenger of their gods. What she always knew but never told, steeped in piety for her brothers, was that her race would be slowly extinguished.

The final night, in his honor, she dressed herself in stars and used the aroma of her alfajores as perfume. Dispersing the clouds to spy better, the Orishás were moved to see her sitting in her hammock, trembling with age, fortified with memories. She was surround by her dead loves who tried to ease her loneliness. And they decided that the time had come. Obatalá, Orishá of all the Orishás, slipped the envoi who would carry her to her place into the abetting night. She would return there with her soul unburdened by having left here the baggage of her actions. And, slowly, her spirit began to come away from her body in which it found a transitory dwelling.

The moon sent waves of light that circled her with incandescence until she glistened with their brilliance.

She was becoming luminous and transparent. And whoever saw her that night of agony would later swear, astonished that unmoving in her hammock María Kumbá radiated an intense rosy glow; and that the light that illuminated her body ascended through the dark firmament, carrying her above its folds until she disappeared, swallowed up by the night.

Come to your Mama, come on, give me your arm, how pretty you are, where were you all this time that you left me all alone? Don't you know, sir, that a woman can never be the same after her children have gone? Why, I even sense the same smell of a nursing calf, my Agustín. Thank you, Yemoja, for keeping him so beautiful for me all this time. I knew you was going to take care of him for me.

My black Manuel! You say I'm jest as good-looking as always? It's your eyes, don't fool yourself. You always saw me pretty, and you was the only one who loved me without such complications. Come on, come on so's I can tell you. All these years that you left me alone a passel of things happened...

How happy you are the two of you being represented to me... I was lucky to have two mamas. All the affection you gave me. Say you're so pleased with me? Proud? Don't go getting me worked up. Why you both taught me everything I knew, and for good or ill I repeated it.

C'mon, youngster, c'mon over here. Don't get jealous on me, shoot. You have to understand me. I'm not used to so many callers. Look at the crowd. Me, without knowing you, I spent my time talking the whole night long. And them, it's been ages since I seen them, and they all have a piece of my heart, bigger or littler. When they left me they took part of my life, the life I was to live with each one. How am I not going to smile at them if it's giving me back life to see them! They didn't forget me. They are coming to get me too. And look here, they made me wait. I also love you. Why, you misspent a whole night with me.

You want me to tell you something? You're not going take me for a crazy woman? Well, I'm telling you... For a big long while I been smelling gunpowder... Yes, I'm not mistaken. You aren't going to learn me what gunpowder smells like. I feel it here in my nose, a mite hot and spiky, it makes you feel like going out to fight...

Thank you, Obatalá, thank you Shangó, I'm not going to

go alone. There are my boys coming now. It's as though I was Auntie María once again. With so much company a body has when you're dying, you can't be sad. With good reason my boys died with a smile. They all came to keep me company. Why you even sent me a messenger, Ifá, so's I wouldn't stray, what with how absentminded I'm being, for sure I was heading off any which way...

Sir Genrul! Why you was the only one missing tonight. How handsome I'm seeing you! Anybody can see you don't suffer any more. Why you even seem younger. Where you been to all this time? Don't go telling me you was resting because I'll get angry. You can't go find somebody else to do what I couldn't do. For sure you went on fighting for the country. Nothing else you know how to do.

You sure did take the biggest piece of my life when you died in my arms so sad. And of course, carrying that secret, how wouldn't it weigh on your soul? Jest say that at the end at least you talked with me about it and doing that always is a relief. But how you suffered, so needlessly—a body dies anyway. C'mon, sit with me. Swear to me that you'll forgive this black woman of yours.

That night I was so angry that I couldn't think and broke all the rules that Mama Basilia had taught me for being an Iyalorishá. Afterwards, I repented each day I stayed alive. And with that I didn't use all the power I know how to use. I only gave a little shove to Tucuman, but without his ever finding out. He did it first. Mama Gervasia told me about it when I heard the news about the commotion the blacks made that night in the Sala. And right there the Ajogún I have inside woke up. Don't look at me that way. Do you know anyone who doesn't have one? Why, not even you're saved from that. I confess to you that night, because of my doubts, I undid Tucuman's work. But the damage had been done. His hatred was greater than my magic. Understand us, Sir Genrul, the two of us got crazy jealous when you made that poor young girl pregnant. It seemed like you'd forgotten about when we was jest the three of us, and mighty happy. You betrayed us, and betrayal has to be paid for. That's jest how it is, no going back. Nobody gets off.

Yes, I know, I'm going to pay for the harm I done too. I began to do it the day you died in my arms. Can you forgive me now? We're too old to tolerate such a load.

Little Virgen del Rosario! Don't you go getting angry on me. I already know that I upset you all my life, but I have to return to the place from whence I came. Shangó sent me to fight and I have to go to account for myself. C'mon, c'mon, youngster, don't be so lumbering any more. We already talked too much and it's going to get light right quick. Once and for all do what you have come to do. I already waited for too long...

EPILOGUE

I am going to conclude this writing. I began it with the last wisp of passion I had left, and it ended as did September. The scent of orange blossoms is killing me.

I fulfilled the pact. Everything I told about what happened is the absolute truth. If you found excesses in my story, they are related solely to my feelings, never to the events I lived through.

I lost years tangled up in dark revenge no one asked of me. Perhaps I was moved by motives hidden so deep that I denied them even to myself. At times it turns out less painful to mask over the truth, never realizing that a half-truth is more dangerous than a lie. No one likes to come up to fear itself. With it you begin a journey from which you do not return.

The final revenge does not go far enough to justify so many years in its service; it is not worth the grief. But it is already late. I ought to have realized before that in reality I loved him from the first moment I saw him, back then in those years at the Colegio. It was the stigma I had to drag around without sharing it with anyone. María always knew. It was sufficient for her to see us together that first day for her eyes to ascertain that she would not have a place in the heart or in the life of her Sir Genrul. I also adored her, and I was the other point on a triangle that time and revenge converted into a game of death and geometry. I loved them both, do not ask me for more, not even if I know how to reply. Man, woman, all that stopped being important to me.

It is my last wish that this writing assist the castigated provinces of the North to survive the ingratitude of time, and the forgetfulness of governments.

Buenos Aires left them to their fate, and when it saw their riches, it brought out its claws.

Where was that mercenary city when people here were

starving to death but saved their coins to make bullets? Looking toward Europe? Watching over power as though it were carrion in order not to share a single piece with us provincial brutes?

Those years were horrible. They continue to be the same today. And we continue to drain each other's blood in fratricidal battles that seem never to end, and we, all of us, drown in that same blood from our useless confrontations. And the Revolution mourns for the countless dead.

Teresa, Antonia, my last smile is for you. In it is my love for your race, a race that with laughter full of white teeth taught me to dance with the joy of being alive. All of them were shamelessly exterminated, as if their blood was not important, their pain too cheap to inventory.

I need to recognize that I already have the habits of the elderly; my eyes are moist from memories. Some time ago, I sent for Juan, her grandson. I want to hand over to him some part of these pages scrawled by a lonely, repentant old man. He needs to know about his grandmother's courage, and to be proud of it. After Belgrano died I knew nothing more about her. In spite of my efforts to find her, she vanished forever from my life. As is known, whoever wishes not to be found becomes invisible.

I believe...better said, I am certain, that she realized I had much to do with his death. She will not be able to forgive the fact that the strength of my hatred was superior to her gods.

Once in awhile news reaches me that she is begging near the cathedral, with a black shawl covering her face. I wish it were not true. I cannot reconcile the image of a beggar with my memory of that much-beloved woman. I was never able to learn for certain if she died or still remains alive. I dare not go to look for her. I could not hold her gaze. I took away from her what she loved most. I left her with her hands full of magic but empty of life. But I took it away from myself too.

Oh, María, how I loved you! I was never able to uproot you from my blood *I vaguely remember the dark, bloody sun that shone behind our eyelids the confusion of colors of feelings was sharp cutting like daggers as if all our senses had melted with our heat confounding our desires happiness that made vertigo immaterial our bodies described slow figures and we touched each other until we accumulated in our tongues avid tribes and races exercised over us an unquiet vigilance my little negrita fluffy dove hot mouth you had us surrender intertwined in the experience as a primitive way of bringing our bodies together each one of us like the moon had its dark side hot little mulatto you outlined that night the shape of unmatched love till the reality broke us like an overly wound spring and the three of us fell to the ground panting just like bewildered birds while our spasms were transmitted under our skin we stayed for a long while like sphinxes of a forgotten action buried in the clay of our faults and around us the silence of the night regained its customary proportions.*

I only reproach you both for the infinite solitude you left me in. You did not absolve me of pain and now I know that my death will be terrible.

Glossary

Terms that are self-defined in the text are not included in what follows.

Adjás: An idiophonic instrument made of an iron bell fixed with a long iron handle.

Ajogún: Diabolical and destructive beings.

Babalawo: Father of the mysteries; highest priest.

Baguala: Folkloric music from Northern Argentina, characterized by a uniform, marked beat. See Vidala.

Batá: Sacred drums.

Buchu: An herb with analgesic and anti-inflammatory properties.

Cencerro: An idiophonic musical instrument. Common cowbell from which the clapper is removed and is struck with a piece of metal or wood.

Chikás: A dance belonging to the tribal cycle of choreography originating in Africa.

Eres: Objects linked to the magical sacred rites.

Erinle: A medical Orishá.

Ewes: Curative herbs and plants.

Idiophonic: The term refers to the production of sound made by the whole instrument.

Ifá: A system of divination that uses Ikin, palm nuts, to make binary patterns, somewhat similar to the I Ching.

Ignomos: Drums used in Macumba that are almost nonexistent

today because their large size makes them difficult to transport.

Iyalorishá: Priestess.

Lonjas: Small ritual drums.

Macumba: The generic term for a group of practices and magical-liturgical rituals that represent a deformation of the Yoruba religion overshadowed by occultism.

Marapós: Percussive instruments of African origin, made up of two small flat strips of wood. When placed between the ring, middle, and index fingers of the right hand and struck, they make a sound similar to castanets.

Marímbulas: A strumming instrument of African origin that is made of a wooden box that serves as a sounding board. Metallic strips on top of the box are plucked by the thumbs, so also "thumb pianos".

Mazacayas: A musical rattle of African origin. It stands on two tin cones joined at the base by a wooden handle used to shake the little pebbles inside to make a rasping sound.

Nagó: The Yoruba language.

Obatalá: Supreme deity of the Yoruba nation; father of the gods.

Oggún: Orishá who cures the heart.

Okó: Orishá of planting.

Olorishá: A devout woman who has already received the ilekes, spiritual beads consecrated by the Orishás and offered to the novices during the initiation ceremony.

Olorúm: The creator.

Ombligada: Typical movement in African dance in which the dancers touch belly buttons.

Omo-Aiye: Malignant human beings.

Ori: The head, the top of things.

Orishás: Yoruba deities, sent to manipulate human nature in order to strengthen it.

Oshún: The Orishá of love and sensuality.

Oyá: The divinity that guards cemeteries and protects the soul of the deceased.

Path-openers: Items used in invoke the different paths, or forms, of the gods.

Pelojilla: A plant material for infusions.

Ronda Catonga: A child's game of African origin.

Sala: A closed hall where Afro-Argentines gathered to carry out liturgical ceremonies.

Tatas Brujos: Old counselors of the African nations.

Tengue-Tengue: The refrain a children's song.

Tulisquín: Powerful poisonous plant.

Tumbá: A drum similar to the conga.

Vidala: Folkloric songs from Northern Argentina, played with a caja, or box, percussion instrument. See Baguala.

Vizachera macho: A grass or weed, Stipa leptostachya Griseb.

Vizcacha empanadas: A savory turnover made with the meat of the vizcacha, a South American rodent, similar to a prairie dog.

Zarabanda: An African dance in which the 6/8 beat and the 3/4 beat are combined.

Curbstone Press, Inc.

is a non-profit publishing house dedicated to multicultural literature that
reflects a commitment to social awareness and change, with an emphasis
on contemporary writing from Latino, Latin American, and
Vietnamese cultures.

Curbstone's mission focuses on publishing creative writers whose work
promotes human rights and intercultural understanding, and on bringing
these writers and the issues they illuminate into the community. Curbstone
builds bridges between its writers and the public—from inner-city to rural
areas, colleges to cultural centers, children to adults, with a particular
interest in underfunded public schools. This involves enriching school
curricula, reaching out to underserved audiences by donating books and
conducting readings and educational programs, and promoting discussion
in the media. It is only through these combined efforts that literature can
truly make a difference.

Curbstone Press, like all non-profit presses, relies heavily on the support
of individuals, foundations, and government agencies to bring you, the
reader, works of literary merit and social significance that would likely not
find a place in profit-driven publishing channels, and to bring these
authors and their books into communities across the country.

If you wish to become a supporter of a specific book—one that is already
published or one that is about to be published—your contribution will
support not only the book's publication but also its continuation
through reprints.

We invite you to support Curbstone's efforts to present the diverse voices
and views that make our culture richer. Tax-deductible donations can
be made to:
Curbstone Press, 321 Jackson Street, Willimantic, CT 06226
phone: (860) 423-5110   fax: (860) 423-9242
www.curbstone.org